SHANE THE COWBOY

By R. J. Robinson

Other Books by the Author:

'Kill Him, Mary!'

A Thousand Years From Now: Thinking Can Get You Killed!

This is a work of fiction. Names, characters, businesses, places, events, locales, and incidents are either the products of the author's imagination or used in a fictitious manner. Any resemblance to actual persons, living or dead, or actual events is purely coincidental.

ISBN: 978-1-7392355-8-1

For

No one in particular

INTRODUCTION

I watched a lot of Westerns when I was growing up in the sixties and seventies. One of my all-time favourites – and still is – was *Shane*, starring Alan Ladd. Indeed, my parents named me after the steely-eyed, calm, cool, and collected, deadly protagonist (thanks, Mum and Dad!).

So, without trying to rewrite what is already a classic Western by Jack Schaefer, I present my up-to-date version of a builder called Shane, not from the Midwest USA, but from the South-East of England, who is a bit of a 'cowboy' and also handy with his weapon.

In my parodic version, however, the premise remains the same, and I drew inspiration from both the original novel and the movie adaptation – I have even used the same character names (except for a few I made up).

In cinemas, nowhere!

CHARACTERS

SHANE: Mysterious stranger and hero

JOE STARRETT: The good-natured but stubborn caravan owner and leader of the Traveller community

MARIAN STARRETT: The great-at-cake-baking, horny, alcoholic wife

ROBERT STARRETT (BOB): Whiny ten-year-old son

LUKE FLETCHER: Greedy property developer and nasty bastard (baddy)

STARK WILSON: Hired gun and a nasty bastard also

SAM GRAFTON: Owner of Grafton's General Store, Beach Bar & Café

JANE GRAFTON: Mr Grafton's rebellious seventeen-year-old daughter and ice cream kiosk attendant

WILL ATKEY: Shit-scared bartender at Grafton's

MELISA ATKEY: Will's much-younger cheating Asian wife, who sometimes works

MR WEIR: Head chef (and only chef) who works at Grafton's café

MORGAN: Fletcher's site manager/enforcer and a big, fat, ugly bastard (baddy)

RED MARLIN: One of Fletcher's 'boys' and a loutish, beer-bellied 'ginger nut' (baddy)

CURLY: Shit-at-fighting, tall and lanky, curly-haired twat and another of Fletcher's 'boys' (baddy)

YOUNG CHRIS: The youngest of Fletcher's 'boys', hot-headed and mouthy (baddy)

BOB TOMKINS: Bent copper

LEW JOHNSON: Frightened Traveller and winger

HENRY SHIPSTEAD: Frightened Traveller and winger

FRANK TORREY: Frightened Traveller and winger

JAMES LEWIS: Slightly less frightened Traveller but still a winger

EARNIE WRIGHT: Thick-as-shit but brave winging Traveller

TRAVELLER WIVES AND CHILDREN: Many

OLLIE JOHNSON: Little Bob Starrett's Traveller pal and a little shit

JAKE LEDYARD: Dodgy travelling salesman (not to be confused with the other Travellers)

THE UGLY SISTERS: Two cruel, fat mingers that aren't actual sisters but look similar and hang around the café a lot together

SPLIFFY: Skinny young lad dating both of the 'Ugly Sisters' and a low-level drug dealer (he's very short)

SAD OLD GIT: Stares out of the café window a lot

ROSIE: The sheepdog

BETSY: The horse

CHAPTER ONE

It was a blisteringly hot summer's day when Shane rode into the quiet seaside town of New Romney in Kent on his beat-up bicycle en route to the beachfront. A place the loner had fond memories of holidaying as a kid. Not much had changed, he noticed. Earlier, he'd caught the Monday 10:29 train from London St Pancras International to Folkestone Central. He then cycled the rest of the way to seek somewhere remote to lie low for the time being. He'd intended to get off at Dover to catch a ferry to France, but mistakenly got off at the wrong stop, then rode in the wrong direction, ending up in New Romney. Still, he thought it would be as good a place as any to hide while things quietened down somewhat. And, besides, by the time he'd have reached the port of Dover, it would've probably been swarming with police in search of him. He thought it ironic that here he was contemplating fleeing to France when hundreds of migrants were coming from there on small boats to these shores.

Before calamity struck, the ex-SAS sergeant's day got off to a good start. He'd polished and off-loaded his bigger-than-average weapon twice during the night. And after kicking out the buxom, blonde-haired sexpot from his modest one-bed rented flat in Dagenham, East London, whom he'd picked up at the local pub the previous evening, he happily cycled off to work early that Monday morning with a great big smile on his face. Unfortunately for Shane, however, his happiness didn't last very long – his bike went slowly uphill, and his day went quickly downhill.

Shane left the British Armed Forces a decorated serviceman, having served two tours of duty in Afghanistan, just under a year ago. Now aged thirty-six, unmarried with no family, he struggled to settle into civilian life, moving from place to place and taking on menial work where he could – which was mainly as a labourer on building sites. However, his employment rarely lasted long, as he would inevitably get fired for his shoddy work or, more often than not, because of his forthright attitude, especially when standing up for his and his fellow workers' rights, which usually involved getting into a fistfight.

Well, today was one such day. Only this time, the fighting went too far, and acting in self-defence, Shane unintentionally caused serious harm to the building site inspector.

No sooner had Shane entered the yard and laid his bike against the muddy ground than he heard the site inspector calling out his name from the construction manager's Portakabin doorway. He was one of those little Hitler types who had it in for Shane the moment he started work there. And by the sound of his voice and the thunderous look on his face, today was no exception.

'You're late again!' moaned the site inspector, tapping his watch.

Then, before Shane could try and explain that as he was cycling up the hill to work, a black cat crossed his path, causing him to fall off his bike, and then had to spend time fixing the chain, the tall, burly inspector came stomping down the steps and started pushing him away, telling him to 'Clear off!' and 'You're fired!' He then started ridiculing Shane, saying his eight-year-old niece could lay a brick wall straighter than him (which, to be fair, wasn't far wrong – he was shit at bricklaying).

Ignoring the childish remarks, Shane – who was only average height with a slim but muscular build – tried to get past him and enter the manager's office to demand his unpaid wages. But the growling beast of a man wouldn't have it and, waving his fists in the air, threatened to hit the much smaller man unless he left. 'Go on – clear off!' he repeated. 'We don't want cowboy builders working here!' which drew guffaws from within the office.

One punch from Shane was all it took: as the angry, potty-mouthed inspector swung a punch at him, he swerved out of the way and, with lightning speed and power, knocked the big guy to the ground unconscious! It was difficult to know whether it was the punch or his head smacking against a concrete slab that did it. But, judging by the increasing pool of blood surrounding the inspector's head, Shane wasn't waiting around to find out – he could've been dead for all he knew. And to the shocked surprise of a few onlookers witnessing what happened, swapping his hard hat for his Stetson, he hastily jumped back on his bike and was off, zooming down the hill.

CHAPTER TWO

Cycling along the quiet sandy beachfront road with only the clothes he wore and a tatty rucksack on his back, containing an empty flask and a half-eaten sandwich wrapped in tin foil, Shane searched for somewhere he might sleep rough for the next few nights or so. Under an upturned rowing boat, perhaps. Or inside one of the few residential properties' unlocked sheds scattered about along the way. The contents of his well-used leather wallet were sparse, too: forty quid and a useless debit card with zero balance and no overdraft facility. He destroyed and threw away his mobile phone at the first opportunity lest the authorities trace his whereabouts.

Shane regretted the unfortunate event earlier, but he acted in self-defence and felt threatened by the man's actions – and it could have been him ending up badly injured instead.

Farther along the long stretch of coastline, looking far out to sea to his left, Shane spotted two tanker ships.

Probably on their way to France or Spain, he thought, wishing he was onboard. Over to his right was a slightly run-down-looking place with a large sign with paint peeling off it above the entrance: Grafton's General Store, Beach Bar & Café. Outside the premises, adding a touch of brightness to the otherwise drab exterior, were colourful Lilos, buckets 'n' spades, and flip-flops for sale. It was busy inside and out, with locals and holidaymakers enjoying lunch or a beer to cool down. And the ice cream kiosk had a queue outside. It felt like stepping back in time.

As Shane rode past, he noticed a group of burly men wearing hard hats staring suspiciously at him. Averting his gaze and resisting the urge to shout, 'What the fuck are you lot staring at!' he continued on his way – he'd had enough trouble for one day. Indeed, upon leaving the armed forces, the war-fatigued veteran vowed never to use violence again. However, it hadn't worked out that way, as trouble seemed to follow him wherever he went.

About a mile ahead, on a large grassy area facing the sea, there were several static caravans in a row. There was a much larger space between two of them, he noticed, suggesting that it was once occupied by another one. Some had children playing outside, and he could hear dogs barking and horses neighing. And directly behind them, less than fifty metres away, was a brand-new luxury housing development site. Straining to look beyond the gaps between the caravans, he saw the company name, Reddishrow, emblazoned on a large signpost. Not a company he'd ever heard of before.

Shane's immediate thought was, I bet the developers aren't too pleased that caravans are blocking the beautiful sea views.

'Darn it!' Shane suddenly said to himself. His chain had come off again. Dismounting his old steed of a racing bike – with its converted Cow Horn handlebars – and using one of the pedals to keep it propped upright, he attempted to fit the limp, rusty chain back onto the cogs. A little over in the distance, he saw a young blonde-haired boy sitting on a white picket fence, seemingly transfixed by him. He began to think that maybe his white Stetson or the steel-capped, brown leather cowboy boots he wore were what was getting the attention. He had to admit, it was a bit unusual.

Wiping the sweat off his forehead with the sleeve of his tan-coloured suede tasselly jacket, the urban cowboy offered the nine or ten-year-old lad a smile and a brief wave, who immediately waved and beamed right back. Behind him, he noticed a tall, well-built man with scruffy brown hair, who he guessed was in his forties, attempting to remove a big tree stump with just an axe.

Shane had just fixed the blessed bike chain for the fourth time that day and was about to get back on his bike when he heard a man's gravelly voice saying, 'Howdy, stranger!' or it could've been, 'Hi there, stranger! You look like you could do with some refreshment!'

Looking up, Shane saw the big man beckoning him to join them while now standing beside the boy, who he assumed was his son, with the axe resting on his shoulder.

Wheeling the bike towards them, Shane lowered his shades, revealing his steely-blue eyes, lifted the brim of his dusty hat, and said, 'Howdy! Don't mind if I do – thanks!'

As he approached the friendly pair at the wooden swing gate to their property, the man held out his hand for Shane to shake, saying, 'My name is Joe – Joe Starrett, and this here' – he put the large palm of his hand over the top of the boy's head and tousled his wild hair – 'is my boy, Robert –'

'My friends call me Bob!' informed the young, smiling lad confidently. Then, offering his little hand, 'Pleased to meet cha! I've never met a real-life cowboy before!' The boy suddenly looked confused. 'But where's your horse?'

Shane shook his hand, too. 'Oh, he's back at the ranch,' explained the slightly eccentric stranger with a widening grin.

'Lemon squash, do you okay ...?' asked Joe, pausing for

the stranger to say his name. 'I didn't catch your name.'

'Shane!' he answered. There was another pause while the big man looked at him enquiringly, expecting to hear his surname, too. 'Just Shane – and lemon squash will do just fine, thanks!'

'Dad! He even talks the way cowboys do!'

Both his father and Shane chuckled.

'Come this way, and I'll get my wife, Marian, to sit down on your face.' At least, that's what Shane thought he heard him say. His hearing wasn't as good since his involvement in active combat, and he had a little trouble understanding the father and son's strong Irish twang.

'Thank you, Joe. That's mighty hospitable of you!' replied Shane, casting such lascivious thoughts aside as he wheeled his bike through the entrance and laid it on the faded fake green lawn.

The small front garden was awash with vibrant colours and a wonderfully scented fragrance as the summer flowers – hydrangeas, geraniums, petunias, wallflowers, sweet peas, candytuft, and rose bushes – growing abundantly along the borders and from ornate hanging baskets attached on either side of the caravan doorway were now in full bloom. It looked as pretty as a picture postcard!

As they approached the large, weathered caravan, Shane could see a sexy-looking, older woman with long blonde hair and full makeup through the window. Catching each other's gaze, the woman smiled widely, displaying her perfectly white 'Turkey teeth', then disappeared.

A moment later, the door to the caravan suddenly burst open, and there she was, wearing hot pants and a tight-fitting t-shirt tied at the waist, showing off her ample assets as she posed in the doorway, framed like an oil painting by a five-year-old.

'Well, who do we have here?' asked Marian with a seductive smile and glint in her eye.

'The name's Shane, ma'am – pleased to make your acquaintance!'

'My – isn't he polite!' she said. 'The menfolk around here aren't usually that polite. So, what's a polite, handsome gentleman like you doing in these here parts?'

Sensing a bit of flirting going on (mainly by his wife, as usual), Joe interrupted the pair. Beginning with a contrived cough, he said, 'Well, I thought Shane looked hot and bothered, so I invited him to come and sit down at our place and said you'd get him a lemon squash before he continued on his way!'

Shane just nodded and smiled.

'Oh, but you must stay for lunch!' insisted Joe's wife. 'I've just cooked a hearty meal – more than enough for all of us! You look like you could do with a good meal inside you?'

'I know what you could do with inside you as well!' mused Shane with a wry smile.

'Oh, go on, Shane – please stay!' whined the boy, pleading with him.

'Well …' began Shane, whose eyes inadvertently settled on his mum's sumptuous breasts.

'My wife's tits are off the menu!' unabashedly joked Joe, patting the stranger heartily on the back before bursting into raucous laughter, followed by even louder guffaws from his sexy wife.

'Joe! Will you stop it!' she implored, blushing and acting coy as she feigned slapping her husband across the face. 'You'll embarrass our guest.' Laughing subsided. 'Shane, I insist!'

Shane looked at Joe as if to say what about you.

'That's fine by me,' said the big man.

'Ple-e-e-se, Shane!' pleaded the boy again, looking up at him with big blue eyes.

'Well, how could I refuse, ' replied Shane, grateful.

'I hope you like a juicy tart!' boasted his wife. 'That's my speciality!'

CHAPTER THREE

After polishing off his generous portion of toad in the hole, the quietly-spoken guest tucked into his steaming hot apple tart and ice cream while Marian fussed over him.

'... Can I get you some more?' Marian asked before he had even finished what he had.

'I'd like some more, please, Marian,' hurriedly said her husband, hopeful.

'You get your own – Shane's our guest,' she snapped back before smiling broadly at Shane again, waiting for his answer.

'Oh, what I have will do me just fine, ma'am!' Shane replied, returning the smile. 'If I eat anymore, I shan't be able to get through the door!'

'Well, alright then. And please call me Marian.'

Shane swallowed another mouthful. 'This is truly delicious, Marian. Thank you kindly!'

'You're welcome, Shane. Isn't he Joe!'

There was a pause before she kicked him under the

table.

'Ow!' *Yes!'* promptly answered Joe, forcing a smile.

'You should try my mum's Cherry Bakewells!' said the boy, licking his lips.

Well, Shane nearly choked on his pastry crust.

During the meal, Joe and Marian (mostly Marian) asked Shane many questions, to which he replied with many evasive answers. However, he did tell them that he was from Billericay, Essex.

He also told them he was single with no children, which caused Marian's eyes to widen. When asked what he did for a living, he told them that he was an out-of-work builder, which brought up the sore subject of the new housing development still being built directly behind them.

'... Those greedy cunts –'

'Joe! Not in front of our Robert!' intervened Marian, tutting.

'Sorry! Bastards!' continued Joe, becoming agitated. 'Those bastards want to take over our land, Shane! Land, we and the rest of the settlers along here paid the farmer for fair and square! All because they want to build more of those fancy homes of theirs closer to the sea. Well, we're not standing for it, are we, Marian?' She shook her head in agreement. 'They'll have to take my body out of here in a wooden box first!' Joe slammed his fist against the table, causing all the uncleared cutlery and plates to rattle like his nerves, frightening their old sheepdog, Rosie (also jobless), who immediately sprang up from its comfortable basket and started barking loudly, plus two steeds, several chickens, and a pig kept out the back.

'Calm down now, honey!' Marian told him, placing a hand on his forearm to placate him. 'Go and play outside, Robert! And take Rosie with you!'

'Oh, but, Mu-um! I want to stay here with Shane!'

'Stop whining and do as your mother tells ya!' said the father sternly.

Sulking, the boy hurriedly left, slamming the rear caravan door shut with a bang.

Continuing the conversation, Marian said, 'They can't take land that's not rightfully theirs! Isn't that right, Shane?'

'Well, I'm no lawyer, ma'am – Marian, I mean – but that sure sounds about right to me.'

'Law or no law – that won't stop Fletcher trying to force us off our land!' stated Joe, a touch calmer.

'Fletcher is the land developer!' quickly explained Marian.

'Has this Fletcher dude been giving you trouble then?' asked Shane, sensing he may have.

'You could say that again,' replied Joe. 'Ever since I refused to accept his measly offer to buy this place, he and his heavies have done their utmost to make life difficult for us poor folk livin' here! He's already caused one family to pack up and leave because of his violent threats!'

'It's the same the world over,' expressed Shane, 'the rich and powerful seem to think they can do whatever they like whenever they like, no matter what the consequences!'

'Too true!' agreed Marian, shaking her head (among other things – her dangly earrings!).

'Well, if their unscrupulous actions continue for much longer, somebody's gonna get killed – mark my words!' worriedly said Joe.

There was an uncomfortably long pause. Then, changing the sore subject, Marian asked, 'So, do you like country and western Music, Shane?' expecting him to say yes.

'No,' simply answered Shane with a shake of the head. Then, after a moment. 'Classical.'

'What – classic country and western music?' she then asked.

'No, just classical – Mozart, Beethoven, Chopin.'

'Oh, I can't stand eighties and nineties Europop bands!' interjected Joe.

Shane just smiled.

'A lot of people say I look a lot like a young Dolly Parton!' said Marian, smiling proudly.

'Yeah, I can see them – I mean, *that,*' replied Shane,

slightly embarrassed as his eyes climbed out of her canyon-like cleavage.

Marian giggled. 'Care for a drop of moonshine, Shane?' she then asked, casually resting her hand on his muscular thigh.

'Oh, no thanks!' he replied, getting up. 'It's been a pleasure meeting y'all, but it's getting late, so I think I best be going now.'

'Oh, Shane – but we've only just got to know you,' began Marian. 'And little Bob will be most upset to see you leave so soon. Won't you at least stay the night? We have a sleeper van out the back –'

'Marian, can't you see that Shane needs to be on his way?'

There was a moment's hesitation before Shane said, 'Well, as long as you are both sure you don't mind.'

'Of course not!' expressed Marian happily. 'Ah, Robert will be very pleased!'

Smiles all around, Marian said buoyantly, 'I'll show you to your quarters where you can freshen up. And, after helping her clear the dirty dishes, he followed her out the back door to the VW camper van, whose four flat tyres suggested it hadn't been on the road for a while. His eyes transfixed on her mesmerising hips as they swayed seductively from side to side, oblivious to the menagerie of animals all around (he had a thing for cougars – especially big-titted blonde ones!).

She unlocked the vehicle and slid the side door partially open. Peering inside, Shane immediately noticed there was a double mattress.

'It could do with a bit of a tidy-up, but I think you'll find it comfortable,' she told him. 'Joe and I had our best sex ever in here!'

Too much information! Shane smiled a little awkwardly without comment.

Then, squeezing through the narrow gap and climbing gingerly onto the slightly manky mattress on all fours, his head brushed unavoidably against her enormous hooters. Giggling, she said, 'Oh, sorry!' and, only then, opened the door wider for him.

'This'll do me fine,' lied Shane. But it was better than the alternative of chancing to sleep uninvitingly in someone's shed. And for that, he was grateful.

'Supper's at eight,' she informed him before turning on her high heels and swaying back the way she came.

CHAPTER FOUR

Later that afternoon, while Joe and Marian were making out in the caravan and Bob was still out playing somewhere, the pair heard a chopping sound out front.

'It sounds like somebody's chopping wood!' said Joe, distracted.

'Oh, nevermind that, Tiger,' groaned his horny wife, 'keep fucking me – don't stop!'

Not wishing to displease his needy wife, he continued screwing her for a bit longer.

'It's no good, Marian,' he suddenly said. 'I need to check who the hell's making that bleedin' racket!

And, to his wife's utter disappointment and frustration, Joe pulled himself out of her and then out of bed (in that order). Then, hurrying to the window with his tool flapping wildly about, he peered tentatively through the curtains and saw Shane swinging a different kind of chopper through the air.

'It's Shane!' Joe announced to his wife. 'He's chopping away at that stubborn tree stump I've been trying to get rid of for months!'

His wife jumped out of bed and ran around to join him, screaming excitedly, 'Let me see! Let me see!' before tripping over Joe's scrunched-up underpants and jeans, he'd left abandoned in a heap on the floor. Reacting quickly, her husband held out his arms and caught her, but in doing so, he accidentally ended up pulling the curtain rail off the wall, resulting in the couple being stark naked in the window for all to see.

Shane did one of those double-takes as if he couldn't quite believe it, as the widely smiling hosts started waving at him.

Sweat pouring off him, Shane averted his gaze and continued hacking at the stump, trying desperately to unsee the image of the naked couple. He looked like a Hollywood movie star, dressed in only his cowboy hat and boots, denim jeans, and Aviator sunglasses, having removed his T-shirt to reveal a well-toned, tanned, and heavily tattooed upper body, glistening in the sun.

'I'd better go and help Shane,' said Joe, quickly getting dressed. 'It wouldn't be right to let him work alone!'

And while her husband went to help Shane, she returned to fulfilling her sexual needs alone on the bed, fantasising about the stranger with the big chopper.

Shane and Joe worked hard all afternoon and into the evening until that big, ugly-looking stump was finally gone. Marian and Bob helped, too, offering the men lemon squash, cookies, and words of encouragement – and while at it, Marian couldn't resist feeling Shane's pumped biceps. She would have offered them a refreshing cup of Rosie Lee if their old electric generator hadn't broken down for the second time that day and they hadn't run out of gas. Rosie did what most dogs do: run around barking noisily in the excitement – especially when the task was complete, and everyone cheered. Thanking Shane, he replied that it was the least he could do for their hospitality.

By the time the work was over, the exhausted, sweat-drenched men had built up a mighty big appetite – even though the only food available was cold tins of chipolatas and baked beans.

CHAPTER FIVE

In the morning, Joe and Marian sat at the breakfast table alone, feeling a bit worse for wear: smoking and drinking strong cups of black coffee after a heavy drinking session the night before. Their somewhat subdued conversation was dominated by discussing their new guest, who had already eaten and was now outside feeding the horses with the help of Bob.

Resting her fulsome breasts on the dining table's edge, Marian suggested, 'I think we should ask Shane if he wants to stay longer. He seems like a nice man, and we could do with more help around here! Our fencing needs securing and –'

'Now hold on a minute, Marian. I thought Shane was quite evasive yesterday, didn't you?' interrupted Joe, keeping his voice down. 'We know very little about him.'

'Well, maybe he's just shy, that's all!'

Lifting one bottom cheek, Joe let off a massive fart. 'It must be those baked beans you served me again for breakfast.'

'I didn't hear Shane complain ... Argh – it stinks!'

'... And didn't you notice all those tattoos and scars Shane had when he was topless yesterday?'

'I sure did,' she answered gleefully.

'The one that stood out to me the most was the winged dagger on the inside of his forearm – I'm sure that's a Royal Marines symbol!'

She snorted a laugh. 'What do you know about the military? The closest you ever got to wearing a uniform was when you had a job as a traffic warden, which, if I remember rightly, you soon got fired from for stealing vehicles!'

'There was a lot of vandalism and theft on my patch, and I was just looking after them for the owners, that's all!' merely remarked Joe with a wry smile before admitting, 'Okay, I confess. I did go joyriding in quite a few of 'em and wrote some off, but I didn't nick any! *Brap!*'

'Anyway – so what if it is a military symbol!' continued his long-suffering wife. 'Maybe he *was* in the armed forces but didn't wanna tell us. He could be suffering from – what's it called? PT ...'

'SD!' offered Joe.

'No – that means sexual disease!'

'Oh!'

'Maybe both,' she muttered, thinking out loud.

'What?'

'Maybe Shane's past is too traumatic to talk about, is what I'm trying to say.'

'Well, that's what worries me a little. What if the lonesome wanderer is dangerous – a psychopath even?'

'Oh, don't be so daft!' instantly said Marian, raising her eyebrows and shaking her head in disbelief.

'We might wake up in the middle of the night dead!'

'What? How d'ya work that one out?' She shook her head again. 'If we're dead, how the bleedin' hell can we wake up?!'

'Well, you know what I mean.'

'No! Honestly – you do come out with a load of crap! I seriously worry about you sometimes! Stop being suspicious about everyone – Shane's a good man!'

There was a pause while Joe reasoned with himself. 'Yes, I believe you're right, Marian.' His face suddenly scrunched up. *'Sssss! Thrrrrp!* Excuse me!'

'Well, that's settled then – we'll ask Shane if he'd like to work for us as soon as he returns!'

Joe nodded his agreement.

Shortly afterwards, a battered old white Transit van pulled up abruptly outside their property, almost smashing into their fence. It was Jake Ledyard, a pushy, long-in-the-tooth travelling salesman about as crooked as his driving.

The driver's door slammed shut. 'Joe – it's that snake, Ledyard!' announced Marian, scrunching up her face.

'Don't let him talk you into buying anything! You hear me?!'

'Oh, hush now, my sweet. I'm only gonna take a quick look at what the man's got – that's all,' replied Joe, heading for the front door.

'Yeah – that's what you said the last time and ended up buying a load of crap – most of which didn't bleedin' work!' she reminded him to deaf ears.

'Top o' the mornin' to ye, Jake!' bellowed Joe as he descended the rickety steps, still wearing his tatty-old dressing gown. *'Brap! Thrrrrp! Parp!'* The big man then headed towards the van, cursing the damned baked beans under his breath. Ledyard was already at the rear, opening the doors. While Marian remained at the caravan doorway, dressed in only her flimsy pink negligee and panties, cross-armed, watching closely as she puffed away on a freshly lit cigarette.

'Morning, Joe!' replied the scrawny-looking salesman with a cheesy grin. 'Looks like it's gonna be another hot one!'

'It sure does,' replied Joe as the pair shook hands.

'Morning, Mrs Starrett!' Moving his head to one side, Ledyard waved to her, maintaining his wide grin while ogling her heavenly tits. She didn't respond, turning her head away instead.

'So, what have you brought for me to look at today? *Brap!'* asked Joe, overly keen as always to find out.

Inside the back of the van were numerous boxes of various shapes and sizes containing all manner of items.

'Well, my friend. I remember the last time we spoke – you mentioned that you were interested in acquiring a new generator.' Joe nodded. 'So, you'll be very pleased to know that it just so happens I have one right here!' Saying this, Ledyard gestured towards a large cardboard box with a flourish. Then, hastily prising it open, he said flamboyantly: 'Feast your eyes on this beauty!' Filled with anticipation, Joe peered inside the box like an excited child on Christmas Day. It's true: Joe had wanted a better, more powerful generator for some time, as their current old one kept breaking down.

'None of your shenanigans, Jake Ledyard!' insisted Marian, sensing he was up to his old tricks. 'D'ya hear me?!'

'Isn't she magnificent?' boasted the slimy salesman, ignoring Joe's wife. 'It's a Hyundai – thirteen litre – low-noise – three-thousand RPM engine – producing an impressive five point three kilowatts of electricity!' All said without another intake of air.

'Well, I dunno. *Thrrrrp!*' uttered Joe, letting another smelly one out. 'It looks expensive – how much is it?'

'We're talking top of the range here – the Rolls Royce of inverter genera—'

'How much?'

'A mere two and a half thousand pounds! A pure

bargain at half the price!'

Joe whistled. 'I don't think Marian would be best pleased if I spent that amount.'

'Well, I tell you what, Joe. Seeing as it's you, I can knock a hundred off the price! How about that?' There was a pause while Joe thought hard about it. 'You won't get it cheaper anywhere else!'

'I take it it's not from off the back of a lorry?!' questioned Joe, coming round to the idea of buying it – gullible as usual! 'And it works okay?'

'No! And, *yes!'* came the dodgy salesman's swift and curt answers (though not necessarily the right way round).

Just then, Shane came into view and headed towards them. *'Parp! Brap! Thrrrrp!'*

'Who's he?' immediately asked Ledyard, looking at the strange-looking man wearing the Stetson with concern.

'Oh, that's Shane. He's our guest,' answered Joe, looking across at Shane as he drew nearer. 'Hi, Shane! *Parp!'*

Steely-eyed, Shane continued staring at the salesman as if about to draw a Colt 45 from his holster. 'A Hyundai – three-thousand RPM engine, you say?'

'Yeah – that's right, mister.'

'It's well overpriced! *Brap!'* stated Shane, poker-faced. There was an uncomfortable silence. 'I sense a bad smell around here.'

You can say that again! thought Ledyard, pulling a face.

'The deal stinks if you ask me! You can buy that exact model online for around thirteen hundred pounds tops!' continued Shane. 'We had one like that on the building site where I worked!'

Joe switched his gaze from Shane to Ledyard as if waiting for him to show his hand in a game of cards.

'Listen, Shaun –' began Ledyard, looking bothered.

'Shane!' interjected Joe, correcting him.

'Listen, mister!' continued Ledyard, struggling to maintain his composure. 'I'd appreciate it if you'd mind your own –' He was about to say 'bloody' but refrained – 'business! This deal is between Joe and me!'

Exhaling a big puff of smoke. 'Don't choo let 'im talk you into buying anything, Joe Starrett – do you hear!' hollered his wife. 'Listen to what Shane's telling you!'

Bob was now leaning up against the side of the caravan, finding the whole thing quite amusing.

'We do need a new generator, dear!'

'Offer the man no more than fifteen hundred – including a bit extra for his trouble!' advised Shane assertively.

Feeling more confident, Joe said, 'Take it or leave it, Jake. That's just about all the cash I've got spare anyway.'

After making a grumbling sound, the unhappy

salesman reluctantly agreed. 'Well, alright then. But you and Butch Cassidy over there can carry the bloody damn thing!'

Joe and Ledyard briefly shook hands and, removing a large wad of cash from his dressing gown pocket, the happy and contented caravan owner paid the man the money. Joe and Shane then lifted the heavy generator off the back of the van before the fuming salesman sped off, yelling through the driver's window, 'This is daylight fuckin' robbery!'

Joe, Marian, and Shane started laughing (and farting). And that's when the couple asked the no-nonsense stranger if he'd like to stay and work for them for a while, which, to all their delight – especially young Bob's – he kindly accepted.

CHAPTER SIX

Soon after Ledyard left with his tail between his legs, Shane helped Joe set up the new generator. Which, despite their initial doubts, worked perfectly well. No more cold baked beans! Yippee-aye-ay! At least for the time being!

A little later that morning, as Shane turned the corner of the caravan on the way to his quarters, he found Marian all by herself, now fully dressed in Primark jeans and a white tight-fitting tee-shirt, leaning against it, smoking a cigarette. She looked sad, and he could tell she'd been crying.

'Howdy, Marian,' said Shane, stopping to see if she was okay. 'Is there something the matter?'

Her eyes found his. 'Oh, take no notice of me – I get a little teary-eyed from time to time. I'll be fine shortly.'

'... Does it have anything to do with the developers trying to kick you off your land?'

She slowly nodded. 'Yeah, mainly, I guess.'

'Well, if you own the deeds, there's not a court in the

land that can take it away from you!'

She snorted a laugh. 'If only that were true.'

'What do you mean?' asked Shane, perplexed-looking.

There was a pause, suggesting she was reluctant to explain.

'... Please don't feel the need to explain if it's gonna make you feel more upset, Marian.' Shane put his hands on her shoulders to comfort her.

Marian smiled thinly, then, after a moment, opened up. 'Joe, in his wisdom, paid cash and bought the land from the farmer on a handshake – that's how the Traveller community does business. So, we have nothing to prove that we own this patch of land! Nothing – not a damn thing!'

'And where's this farmer?'

'Spain was the last I heard.'

'Spain!' merely repeated Shane with a slight frown.

'I warned Joe, but would he listen ...?'

Shane could see that Marian was getting worked up and teary again. 'Try not to worry, Marian. I'm sure things will work out just fine –'

'Pretty much all our savings went into this place' – she began to sob – 'and if we lose it, I don't know what we'll do!'

Marian reached inside her low-cut tee, giving Shane an eyeful, and pulled out a crunched-up tissue to wipe her eyes (she had a lump in her throat, and he had a lump in his pants).

Struggling with what to say next to the anguished host that he hadn't already said before, he let her continue speaking. 'Shane – I'm sorry. It's not fair of me to burden you with my troubles.'

'Oh, don't worry about that!'

Looking down at her soaking wet tissue, which had make-up smears all over it, she then began to chuckle. 'Oh, my make-up's all smudged. I must look a right mess!'

'No, no. You look ...' Shane was going to say beautiful, but thinking better of it, said, 'Fine!' instead.

There was no mistaking the sexual tension between them, but if there was one thing the military had taught him, it was self-discipline. He was a guest in the Starrett's home and, therefore, should act accordingly by behaving respectfully, even if the landlady wasn't.

Gaining her composure, she asked, 'Do you ride, Shane?'

'Sorry!' he replied, unsure at first what she meant. Then, removing his mind from the gutter, he answered, 'Oh, *horses!* Yeah, I do!'

'There's nothing I like more than to get myself up at the crack of dawn and gallop completely naked along the water's edge!'

Too much information! Shane thought, cocking an eyebrow.

'Why don't cha come and join me sometime?' continued Marian, much cheerier.

'Love to!' he replied, thinking, now what have I gotten myself into? Noticing her sudden change of mood, he said, 'Right, well, I'd better get myself washed. See you later, Marian.'

'Yeah, see you later, cowboy!' she replied with a wink before they parted company. *'... Oh, Shane!'*

'Yeah!' He stopped and turned, thinking, *Crap – what now!*

'Please don't tell Joe about me getting upset, will you? He worries enough as it is!'

Shane gave her a reassuring smile. 'I promise!' he said before continuing on his way with an even bigger lump in his pants.

CHAPTER SEVEN

The school summer holidays were in full swing, and a cacophony of sounds filled the warm sea air: kids screaming and shouting, laughing and crying; builders sawing, hammering, and drilling, along with their powerful noisy vehicle engines; and a menagerie of animals and seabirds adding to the clamorous mix; oh, and Marian's frequently loud orgasms. Apart from that, it was pretty quiet!

Shane kept reasonably busy all week, helping Joe erect tall fences around the rear and side perimeters of the property. Shane also managed to keep himself out of trouble for a change and had yet to venture beyond the immediate area, believing it wise to maintain a low profile still. However, his resolve was about to be tested when, on Saturday morning, around ten-ish, a black, top-of-the-range Range Rover pulled up outside the caravan in a cloud of dust.

Joe was halfway under his old silver BMW saloon car (one he still denies nicking during his days as a traffic warden), parked at the side of the caravan, trying to fix a mechanical problem. Shane and the boy were running around playing 'cowboys and Indians', while Marian was baking cakes.

Stepping out of the flashy vehicle first was the wealthy property developer, Luke Fletcher – age fifty-six, average build and height with dyed blonde shortish hair, sharply followed by four of his 'boys' (or henchmen, as some would call them): 'Morgan' (Fletcher's right-hand man) – age forty-two, big and tall with short black hair, 'Red Marlin' – age thirty-eight, tallish and overweight with straggly red hair, 'Curly' – age twenty-seven, tall and lanky with long curly brown hair, 'Young Chris' – age twenty-two, slim and of average height with short fair hair. A mean bunch of ugly mother-fuckers if ever there were!

'Fuckin' dog shit!' cussed Curly, stepping right into a big pile of it.

Young Chris began to laugh.

'Shut the fuck up!' ordered Morgan before the doors slammed shut, and all five approached the property with only the flimsy white picket fence separating them.

Blackened face and hands, Joe slid from under his vehicle, spotting who it was from his horizontal position with immediate dismay. Shane and Bob stopped in their tracks before Shane told the boy to go and play around the back. Looking out of the front kitchen window,

Marian let out a yelp and dropped the cake she had just baked onto the vinyl floor.

Standing in a straight line with the boss in the middle, dressed in smart suits and shades, looking more like Mafiosi than construction workers, the Starretts stared at them in dread. Not Shane – he feared no one.

Standing up, Joe spoke first:

'What do you want, Fletcher?'

Fletcher snorted a laugh. 'Well, that's no way to treat a neighbour. I come in peace –'

'Is that why you brought your heavies along with ya?'

Sensing the situation was about to get ugly, Shane scoured the garden for potential weapons while remaining calm and collected where he stood.

'I was hoping that you'd seen sense and changed your mind about selling me this plot of land –'

'Well, you and your boys could have saved yourself a journey because my answer is the same as last time –'

'Now you listen to me, Starrett,' spat Fletcher, quick to anger. 'I offered you and the rest of the low-life squatters along here a fair deal, which is a lot more than you say you paid for it. Now either accept my generous offer or suffer the consequences!'

Just then, Marian stepped into the open doorway, looking angry with a frying pan in one hand and a rolling pin in the other, shaking nervously.

'Oooh! I'm scared!' pretended Curly with much

exaggeration, putting his fingers in his mouth and shaking his knees wildly about.

'Listen, Fletcher,' fumed Marian, 'if you think your threats and pathetic intimidation tactics will cause us to leave as they did with the other Traveller family, you are very much mistaken!'

'Oh, go back inside, woman – this is men's talk!' responded Fletcher harshly.

Shane cooly stepped forward, pushing the brim of his Stetson upward, and began addressing Fletcher. 'Now, looky here, mister –'

'Look out, boys!' Red Marlin hurriedly called out. 'Here comes the fuckin' sheriff!' which caused much merriment among Fletcher's gang. Chris doubled over in hysterics.

'– You can't just go round threatening people like that!' continued Shane, undaunted. He had met their type before, working on the building sites, so their uncouth behaviour was nothing new. 'You heard what the man said. So why don't cha get back in your fancy car and leave!'

Fletcher's gang all looked at each other as if wondering what to say or do next.

'You tell 'em, Shane!' shouted little Bob, who had just appeared from around the side of the caravan.

Fletcher scoffed. 'I *own* most of this *fuckin'* town! And soon I'll own all this area of prime real estate as well. So,

I'll do and say whatever I goddamn *fuckin'* like!' hollered the developer as he glared at Shane.

Meeting his aggressive gaze, Shane quickly responded with, 'Hey! Hey! Less of the swearing – there's a child present!' and he had to do everything in his power to stop himself from rushing over and punching Fletcher's lights out.

'Yeah! Don't swear, you fuckin' wankers!' shouted little Bob before looking sheepishly towards his parents as if to ask, am I in trouble now?

'Well, you've had your chance, Starrett. Don't say I didn't warn ya!' growled Fletcher. 'And it was a waste of time putting up all that fencing – 'cos that'll all be coming down as soon as I take ownership! Come on, boys! Let's go – it stinks around here!'

More unkind laughter ensued. Then, before turning to follow the boss, Morgan formed his hand into a pistol and made a shooting gesture toward Shane before raising his two extended fingers to his mouth as if to blow away the smoke. Two others thought it funny to kick sections of the pretty picket fence over, damaging Marian's beautiful hydrangeas.

'BEGONE WIT'CHA – YA BASTARDS!' angrily screamed Marian, raising her cooking implements.

'Where d'ya think you're fuckin' going?' Morgan suddenly asked Curly as he was about to step into the back of the Range Rover. 'You're not coming in here with that stinking shit on your shoes!'

Young Chris and Red Marlin burst out laughing.

'But how am I gonna get back?' the tall, skinny lad, whose suit was two sizes too big and looked like it was about to fall off him, asked.

'Fucking walk! You wanker!' came the site manager's blunt reply.

The rear door slammed shut to more laughter as Young Chris mockingly waved him goodbye. Then, the Rover sped off in a cloud of dust once more and disappeared.

As soon as Fletcher and his boys left, Marian dashed back inside and burst into tears.

Joe looked at Shane as if to ask what to do. 'Go and comfort her, Joe. Reassure her that everything's gonna be all right,' offered Shane. 'They're just a bunch of idiotic thugs, that's all. Hopefully, they'll soon grow up and see reason.'

Joe nodded and moved swiftly towards the caravan door.

'Come on, Bobby-boy!' next said Shane. 'Let's go and feed the livestock!'

CHAPTER EIGHT

It took Joe the rest of the morning to console Marian. Such was the torment and stress caused by Fletcher and his boys. Which, of course, was their aim. It had worked with one of the other Traveller families, who had upped sticks in the middle of the night a couple of weeks back, fearing for their welfare, leaving an unfavourable open space where their caravan once stood in their wake.

Indeed, the fear was so great that most Travellers dared not leave their homes in case Fletcher torched them. A threat he had made on more than one occasion!

'... What are we going to do?' Marian desperately asked her husband once the sobbing had stopped and she'd calmed down a little. 'I dread to think what would've happened if Shane hadn't been here and stood up for us as he did!'

Joe nodded and said, 'Well, I think you did a pretty good job yourself, Marian.'

She just sighed and rested her head upon his well-rounded shoulder.

'We must remain strong and not give in to those bullies,' advised Joe before adding, 'I will arrange a meeting with the other families this evening. We will be stronger if we remain united!'

The other families of Travellers looked up to Joe Starrett and saw him as their leader.

In the meantime, Joe got to work, fixing the broken picket fence and tidying up the flower bed as best he could. Low on nails, he asked Shane if he'd fetch some more from Grafton's.

'Sure thing!' replied Shane.

'Just ask Sam Grafton to put the goods on my tab.'

'Will do.'

'Can I come with you, Shane?' keenly asked Bobby-boy, smiling widely.

'Well ...' hesitantly began Shane.

'Bob, stop bothering Shane. Can't you see he's busy?' his mum called out from the open kitchen window while doing the washing-up, which had piled up from breakfast and lunch. 'Come inside and do your schoolwork.'

'But M-u-u-m – it's the school holidays!' protested the young lad, whose smile had quickly morphed into a scowl.

'I don't care! It's more important that you study hard so you don't end up like your father –'

'Oi! I heard that!' voiced her husband from where he squatted next to the flowerbed. 'Go on, Son. Do as your mother tells ya.'

And while Bob stomped begrudgingly up the caravan steps, Stetson-wearing Shane wheeled his bike through the gateway and onto the dusty and bumpy road to ride to Grafton's.

Shane hadn't gone far when he heard Bob running behind him, calling out his name. 'Shane! Wait for me!' No sooner had the lad entered his bedroom and slammed the door shut behind him than he opened the window overlooking the rear garden and climbed out, sneaking around the caravan before scampering off while his parents weren't looking.

Shane stopped and waited for the boy to catch up. 'Bob! What are you doing here?'

'My parents said it was all right!' lied Bob, as if butter wouldn't melt in his mouth.

After a moment's thought, 'Well, alright. Jump on the back. I guess this won't take long,' said Shane, not buying the lad's bullshit for a minute. 'But when we return, I suggest you sneak back into the caravan the way you came so your parents aren't cross.'

Smiling sheepishly, the boy nodded, and the two set off again. Shane chuckled to himself – the boy reminded him of himself when he was his age.

As they rode past the other Traveller's caravans,

children came to greet them by the side of the road and waved. To entertain the children, Shane had attached colourful ribbons – which Marian gave him – to the back of his bike to resemble a horse's tail.

'Bob! Who's that you're with?' called out Bob's friend Ollie Johnson, curious.

'This is my new friend, Shane! He's a real cowboy!'

'Oh, yeah? Well, if he's a cowboy, how come he doesn't have a horse?' challenged his instantly jealous friend.

''cos he left it back at his ranch. Didn't you, Shane?'

Shane nodded. 'Yeah!'

'What's his name?' Shane quickly asked Bob.

'Oh, that's Ollie.'

'Nice to meet you, Ollie!' Shane called out as he rode past.

Stepping onto the road, Ollie shouted out: 'PAEDO!'

A short while later, Shane and the boy dismounted the bike outside Grafton's, leaving it by the sandy roadside before venturing inside. By now, it was mid-afternoon, and compared to lunchtime, it was much quieter.

As the boy rushed inside, ever alert and always on the lookout for danger, Shane remained momentarily at the doorway while he surveyed the large interior. His years of military training and active combat service had conditioned him to be this way.

Sitting in the café to his left, staring wide-eyed at him

while slurping the remains of their strawberry milkshakes, were two obese young women who looked like sisters. Both had long blonde hair, wore matching floral dresses, and bright red lipstick. At a separate table sat an old, wizened-looking man with a scraggy white beard who stared aimlessly through the wide glass frontage out to sea. In the bar area, over to his right, was a group of raucous construction workers huddled around a table, drinking and playing cards.

Despite being more aware of the loud construction workers, he couldn't help but notice, however, how rude the two young women were to the frail-looking old man. The foul-mouthed pair began taunting him about his smell. 'I wish he'd hurry up and fuckin' die so we don't have to smell him!' said one of them, to which they both cruelly laughed.

The sad and lonely old man lived in a small bungalow nearby, and since his wife passed a few years ago, he had let himself go.

Heading straight ahead towards the general goods store, Shane stopped by the small hardware section and picked up two boxes of four-inch nails before continuing to the counter at the rear.

There, a friendly face greeted Shane. 'Another beautiful day in paradise!' said the middle-aged owner, Sam Grafton, with a warm smile as he scanned the items.

'Sure is,' replied Shane, returning the smile.

'Are you on holiday?'

'No-no,' began Shane before turning his head to see where Bob was. He was looking at a child's sheriff costume, complete with a waistcoat and hat, a pistol and holster, and, of course, a star-shaped shiny silver badge, hanging up on a partition in the limited toy section, 'I'm working for the Starrett's.'

As soon as Shane mentioned that name, Mr Grafton's demeanour changed completely. He suddenly looked concerned, quickly glancing towards the bar where the group of men remained. Then, returning his attention to Shane, he remarked with suspicion, 'Oh, yes. I've heard about you.'

Jake Ledyard, the travelling salesman, had been mighty quick to spread venomous gossip and lies about his encounter with the newcomer. Painting him out to be belligerent and troublesome. Not that the locals paid too much attention to what Ledyard had to say – they all knew the type of character he was. But mud sticks – especially in a small town – and it wasn't long before tall stories and vicious rumours about the mysterious stranger had manifested on many a local tongue.

'That'll be five pounds fifty!' hurriedly continued Grafton, as if he couldn't wait to get rid of him.

'Oh, yes, and that toy – bring it over, Bob!' beckoned Shane, seeing how much the boy wanted it.

Beaming, the boy grabbed the package from the wall and hurried towards his hero. Placing it on the counter, the boy immediately hugged Shane and said, 'Oh, thank you, Shane! Now I can be like you!'

The owner looked at the pair in bewilderment. Rarely had he seen such mutual affection! The so-called 'mysterious stranger' standing before him was hardly the type of person Ledyard and a couple of Fletcher's boys had depicted. Regardless, he hastily put Shane's crumpled-up cash in the till and gave him his change.

Just then, a man suddenly appeared from behind the bar via a connecting doorway. It was Will Atkey, the barman, a nervy-looking, short and skinny fella with sparsely combed-over dyed black hair and a little moustache, probably in his mid-fifties.

'Have you seen my lazy ... wife?' Atkey nearly swore but refrained when he saw customers there. His much younger, attractive Asian wife, Melisa, had sneaked off into the kitchen storeroom with the head chef, Mr Weir, who was banging her from behind while she leaned over the stack of potato sacks with her short skirt up around her waist and her knickers wedged aside by his big fat sausage. Their groaning and grunting were drowned out only by the sounds of loud banter from the bar, the noisy ice cream maker, and the up-tempo beat of a Steps track – which was often the pair's secret cue to go and have a quick shag.

The owner quickly shook his head.

'Would you like an ice-cold bottle of Coke, Bob?' asked Shane, pocketing the nails and handing Bob his gift.

'The café's closed!' sharply advised Grafton, remaining cautious.

'That's okay!' responded Shane just as quickly. 'I see the bar is still open – I'll get one from there.' He then leaned towards the boy. 'Bob – you wait out the front while I get your Coke. I won't be long.'

Lost for words, the owner used his head instead to gesture for the barman to return behind the bar and serve the undeterred customer.

As Shane calmly strode under the large archway and into the bar area, the noise from inside suddenly stopped. Approaching the well-worn, wooden bar with his back towards the muted group, he could sense four sets of eyes bore into the back of his head, and, as he leaned against it, catching a glimpse of their reflection in the bar's mirror confirmed it. He recognised two of them from earlier. And judging by all the uncleared empty pint glasses on their table, these fellas had had quite a skinful.

'W-w-what can I g-g-get you?' asked the stuttering barman, clearly nervous and expecting trouble having realised who he was.

'Just a bottle of Coke,' replied Shane. There was sudden laughter. Then Shane heard a grating noise as one of the wooden chairs slid against the wood-effect laminate floor, followed by footsteps approaching the bar.

'Say, mister – aren't you the same fella I saw at the Starrett's caravan earlier?' Shane heard the approaching man's voice ask, slurring his words slightly. Red Marlin.

'Give him what for, Red!' he heard another man say. Young Chris.

Shane casually turned to face Red, remembering that he was one of the dastardly culprits who kicked the picket fence onto Marian's cherished flowers. He was now wearing a construction worker's outfit with his yellow hard hat skew-whiff upon his head, exposing tufts of red hair, and he held a three-quarters-full pint of lager, which swilled around erratically as he wobbled about unsteadily.

Shane looked him right in the eye. 'Yeah – that's right. What about it?'

The bigger man shifted his gaze towards his sniggering buddies and, smirking, remarked, 'I thought so. I smelt him as soon as he moseyed in!' to which the others cruelly burst out laughing. It felt to Shane that he was back in the schoolyard again. And the one thing he'd learnt about bullies is to retaliate immediately, or they'll only keep bullying. He discovered that the hard way! He could feel the anger rising inside him. But as much as he wanted to beat the shit out of every one of them, he was mindful he had Bobby-boy in his care.

Bob was outside, peering wide-eyed through the window, watching all the commotion inside unfold, vying for his hero to unleash hell.

Much to the lad's disappointment, ignoring Red Marlin's offensive remark, Shane turned his back on him and asked the barman, 'How much?'

'It's on the house,' nervously replied the barman, as he shakily prised off the bottle top and plonked the frothing bottle of Coca-Cola onto the bar before dashing away quickly.

Shane heard the uncouth thug beside him belch, then scoff and say, 'Why don't you prefer a manly drink?' which he ignored.

'Are you gay?' suddenly asked mouthy Young Chris, provoking him further.

To more intimidating laughter, Shane casually turned around again and, unflinching, answered: 'Why – d'ya wanna kiss?' Which caught the cocky lad off guard and left him speechless for a change.

Outside, the boy struggled to hear his quiet, evenly spoken hero through the glass. He could only hear the loud, brash voices and raucous laughter of the 'baddies'.

'He looks like one of the "Village People"!' then remarked Red Marlin mockingly as he flipped his wrist in a camp gesture to an eruption of laughter and loutish behaviour from the table.

Shane quickly retorted, 'Well, you would know – dressed as a construction worker!' Shot from the hip, as it were.

The laughter suddenly stopped, and instantly losing his sense of humour, the beer-bellied builder took a well-telegraphed swipe at Shane. Shane ducked and, losing his balance, the drunkard fell flat on his arse, spilling the remains of his Heineken all over himself. Cursing with embarrassment, he tried to get up but couldn't.

Sam Grafton then suddenly appeared behind the bar. 'I don't want any trouble in my establishment – do you hear!' he called out to those who'd listen.

'Come and fight me!' angrily called out Young Chris, getting up before one of his work colleagues pulled him back down to his seat.

Then, as Shane calmly picked up the bottle of Coke and walked away, he heard Red Marlin's irate voice shout: 'THAT'S IT – FUCK OFF! IF I EVER SEE YOU AGAIN, I'LL FUCKIN' KILL YA!'

As Shane exited the premises through the cafe entrance amid stares from the two 'Ugly Sisters' again, who were now stuffing their faces with ice cream, he saw Bob sitting on the porch, looking glum.

'Hey – I've got you a Coke, Bob!' expressed Shane, trying to remain upbeat and not let those bastards inside get the better of him. But the boy refused to take it, gesturing for him to keep it before turning his head away in a snub. 'What's the matter ...' Shane began enquiring before suddenly realising his bike was no longer where he'd left it. 'Where's my bike!' he asked instead.

The boy just shrugged, still not speaking.

'Someone's nicked it!' expressed Shane, looking hastily around, annoyed. 'Come on! We'll have to walk back!'

Shane started walking, still holding the unwanted Coke bottle, still unsure why Bob was upset. Probably the stolen bike, he assumed. But that's not why Bob was feeling down: it was because his hero had let those bullies walk all over him without a fight – at least in his eyes – certainly not how he'd seen it play out in the movies!

Bob followed shortly, head down and empty-handed: he'd tossed the Sheriff's outfit gift from Shane in the rubbish bin outside.

CHAPTER NINE

During the tiring march back in the blazing heat, Shane and Bob hardly spoke. Neither was very happy: Shane, because, apart from having his bike stolen, felt he had shown weakness, allowing his tormentors to continue ridiculing him by not putting a stop to it right away. And, Bob, because the hero he had built up so highly in his head, had turned out not to be a hero after all – though it didn't take long before the thirsty lad did accept the bottle of Coke from him.

Fewer children greeted them on the way back. And the naughty boy, Ollie, was nowhere to be seen.

'It could be worse, Bob,' commented Shane, trying to cheer the lad up without much success as sweat poured off him. 'At least whoever it was didn't steal my stallion!'

If you even have a horse, the disillusioned boy began to wonder.

Upon Shane and the boy's arrival back at the caravan, Joe and Marian greeted the slightly weary-looking pair.

They were cosied up together in a two-seater swing chair by the caravan, now dressed in skimpy beachwear that left nothing to the imagination, smothered in oil, tanning themselves, and drinking beer. Indeed, the weather forecast showed it would continue to be scorching hot for at least another week.

'What took you so long?' asked Joe.

'More importantly! Robert – why aren't you in your room studying?!' questioned Marian.

Shoving the gate open and ignoring his parents, the upset boy shot past them and rushed into the caravan.

'Whatever's happened?!' asked Marian, concerned.

'And where's your bike?' suddenly asked Joe, noticing it was missing.

'Everything's fine!' Shane began reassuring them. 'While we were at Grafton's, I ran into a spot of bother with a few of Fletcher's boys. Drunk as a skunk they were!'

'That doesn't surprise me!' quickly interjected Marian, as she took a big swig of beer.

'But nothing I couldn't handle!' continued Shane. 'And then, as we left, I noticed somebody had pinched my bike.'

'Those bastards!' said Marian, shaking her head. 'When will they ever stop?!' She then quickly got up and went to check on her son – her day-glow green bikini bottoms swallowed up by her ample arse cheeks, which were now fully exposed. She was as hot as a sports car bonnet in the midday sun and had curves to match!

'Leave him, Marian. Stop fussing over the lad!' said Joe. But she ignored him and carried on inside anyway. Then returning his attention to Shane. 'D'ya want me to call the police and report it stolen?'

'No – no,' voiced Shane, quick to reply, prising his eyes off of Marian's arse. 'It's not worth much!'

'The cops probably won't do much anyway – they never do around here! They're about as useless as my dick once I've shot my load!'

Too much information! thought Shane immediately – a phrase he found himself repeating a lot while in the company of the Starretts.

'Did you get the nails?' asked Joe, changing the subject to Shane's relief.

'Yeah.' Shane reached into the side pockets of his jacket and handed them over to his boss. 'Here ya go!'

'Thanks,' said Joe with a smile. 'Did you put them on my tab?'

'No, I paid cash.'

'Oh, ya shouldn't have done. No problem – I'll square up with you later!' The slightly red-chested bear of a man then got up, adjusting his red Speedos as he did. 'Well, I guess I'd better finish putting those blessed fences back up. A happy wife is a happy life, as they say!' There was a pause while both men chuckled. 'Oh, by the way, Shane. I've called a meeting with my fellow Travellers after dinner this evening. Join us if you like!'

'Sure!' answered Shane with a nod.

That said, Joe got to work while Shane sauntered around the back of the caravan for a siesta.

Now wearing her baby pink towelling bathrobe, Marian found her son sobbing in his room. 'Why are you so upset?' she asked caringly as she sat beside him on the bed. Reluctantly at first, he then began to explain:

'... Shane just stood there and did nothing while those horrible men picked on him, Mum. Like he was scared of them!'

'Oh – no – I doubt that very much, Bob. Not Shane!'

'So why did he let them get away with it then?' he questioned as he looked up at her with his wet, bulging blue eyes, searching for an answer.

'Well ... I'm sure he had his reasons, Son,' was the best answer she could give. 'Try not to let it bother you. Now, please do a bit of studying, you little rascal.' She started tickling him, which caused the lad to giggle wildly.

'Mum! Stop it!' he quickly protested, wriggling about on his side. 'MUM!'

'Promise me you'll do it!' said his mum as she continued tickling him.

'I PROMISE! I PROMISE!' he screamed.

She stopped, kissed him on the head, and, getting up to leave, said, 'I'll make you a nice cuppa!'

Smiling, he replied, 'Thanks, Mum!'

She stopped in the doorway and, turning to face him, said delicately, 'Bob – it's best that you don't let yourself get too close to Shane. I know you like him a lot, but he probably won't be staying for much longer.'

Bob's smile dropped a little, and he remained still for a moment as if deep in thought, then gave her the briefest of nods before leaning over the side of his bed and picking up one of his many schoolbooks strewn across the floor.

A little later, when Marian was alone with Joe in the kitchen, she spoke to him about the incident at Grafton's earlier in the afternoon:

' ... You should never have asked Shane to fetch those nails!' remarked Marian, slightly peeved. 'You know that Fletcher's boys are always hanging around Grafton's.'

'Well, the fences weren't gonna bleedin' fix themselves, Marian!' countered Joe, sensing his wife was trying to pin the blame on him for what happened.

'What I mean is ... you should've got off your lazy arse and gone and got them yourself!'

'That's it, blame me! Like you always do!'

'I do blame you – I blame you for not thinking as usual!'

The conversation started to get heated.

'Shane's big enough to take care of himself. He's

probably fought in far worse danger zones before!' he said, sniggering.

'Well, according to our son, he just stood at the bar like a cowardly chicken while Fletcher's boys abused him!'

'Nah – really?'

'Yeah – really!'

Well, what was he doing in the bar anyway?'

'He was kindly treating our son to a bottle of pop. My point is: it's not fair to expect Shane to put up with the same shit we have to put up with and fight our battles for us – especially if he has fought in armed conflicts before. He probably came here looking for solace and peace.'

'Well, he's come to the wrong godforsaken place!' interjected her husband. Said unintentionally glib. Joe was never one to choose his words carefully!

She gave him a thunderous look.

'Not since Fletcher reared his ugly head around here, anyway,' continued Joe after a beat. 'Look! I appreciate Shane helping us as much as you do, but let's be realistic: if he stays with us, it'll be impossible to avoid trouble. Especially with Fletcher and his boys set on turfing us out!'

With a look of dismay, Marian nodded before heading to the kitchen to start preparing the evening meal.

CHAPTER TEN

For whatever reason, Shane didn't come to dinner that evening. Marian called out to him more than once but received no response. 'I expect he's sleeping, Marian,' Joe told her. 'Leave him be.'

With the dinnerware cleaned and stored away, the hosts welcomed the first of their fellow Travellers into their humble abode for a meeting.

As usual, Lew Johnson was the first to arrive. He was wheeling Shane's bike, which his son, Ollie, had nicked while Shane and Bob were inside Grafton's earlier that day.

Joe and Marian greeted the old timer warmly. He and his large family were among the first to stake a claim, as it were, on the farmer's plot.

'... I believe this bike belongs to your new helper,' said the grey-bearded, sixty-eight-year-old man as he leaned the dusty old bike against the caravan. 'My little shit of a son, Ollie, thought he'd help himself to it.'

'I thought it looked familiar,' commented Marian,

straining a little in the remaining daylight. 'Shane'll be pleased!'

'I hope you gave your lad a good telling off!' said Joe somberly.

Lew nodded. 'And I gave him a good clip round the ear and sent him off to bed early!'

Henry Shipstead arrived shortly after. He was also getting on in years and was one of the early settlers who put down roots there.

Slightly late, Frank Torrey, James Lewis, and Earnie Wright noisily arrived as a group and crammed themselves through the narrow caravan door. These were all younger men in their thirties and forties.

An array of glasses was quickly dispensed among the men before Marian sank her teeth into the cork of a tatty old, recycled bottle of liquor vaguely resembling whisky, yanked it out and filled their glasses. And, on this occasion, she was a little more respectfully dressed, swapping her skimpy bikini for a low-cut blouse and miniskirt instead.

Sat or stood wherever they could find in the open plan lounge and kitchen, glasses clinked, while two or three quickly and quietly muttered the Hail Mary to themselves. Then, after releasing a mighty cough, big Joe Starrett spoke: 'Fellow Travellers! Thank you for attending this meeting ...'

Marian swiftly downed her glass and quickly poured

herself another, sensing tension among the group.

'... I've said it before, and I'll say it once more: there is strength in numbers! As you know, one of the families has already left – and if more of us follow suit, it puts those choosing to remain in a much weaker position –'

'Yeah, well, I've already made up my mind,' interrupted Frank Torrey. 'My wife, ten kids, and I are leavin'! And there's nothing you – Joe – or anyone else here can say to make me change my mind. We're not waiting around here for our home to be burnt to a cinder or for any of us to be seriously injured or killed! And if you fools had any sense, you'd pack up and leave too!'

As he spoke, Joe closed his eyes briefly, disappointed. Then, as he opened his mouth to speak again, Earnie Wright started making chicken noises instead.

'I ain't no chicken!' immediately voiced Torrey. 'And if any of you think otherwise, I'll meet you round the back ' – he raised his fist – 'and fuckin' convince you otherwise!'

'I'll fight you any time you fuckin' like!' replied Wright, getting out of his chair. As with the rest of them, all spoken in a thick London-Irish accent.

Unable to sleep with all the excitement and noise, Bob Starrett quietly pulled his bedroom door ajar to listen to the arguing down the narrow hall.

Raising his voice, Joe intervened. *'Hey!* We'll have no

such talk here! Save your anger for Fletcher and his boys!'

'Well, skinny features fuckin' started it!' protested Torrey, referring to Wright teasing him – a tall, bony fella who often acted without thinking.

'Well, I'm fuckin' ending it!' angrily stated Joe, wanting to bang their bleedin' heads together.

Little Bob wasn't the only one eavesdropping that evening. Hearing the commotion, Shane left the camper van and was now standing below an open window of the caravan, debating whether to go inside and properly introduce himself.

'Speaking of cowardice!' uttered James Lewis. 'I happened to be in Grafton's this afternoon. Picking up some putty to replace a broken window, which one of Fletcher's boys was no doubt responsible for –'

'Ah, that might have been little Ollie,' suddenly admitted Lew Johnson, slightly embarrassed. 'I meant to tell you about that.'

'Go on!' Joe urged Lewis, wanting to hear what he had to say, suspecting it was about Shane.

'Well, when I arrived, I could hear Fletcher's drunken louts taking the piss out of someone in the bar. So, curious, I went and took a peek. And there he was – the cowboy –'

'Shane?' interjected Marian.

'Yeah – that's the dude! He just stood there and did

nothing –'

Suddenly, Bob appeared, dressed in his Incredible Hulk pj's, and shouted, 'IT'S TRUE!'

'Robert! Go back to your bedroom now!' ordered his mum.

'Ooooh – it's NOT fair!' Bob complained, disappointed, before turning reluctantly on his heels and obeying her.

There were a few titters among the group. Then, picking up the thread of conversation again, Marian suggested, 'Well, maybe Shane's tired of fighting – Joe thinks he was in the army!' which seemed to fall upon deaf ears.

'I would've beat the shit out of em', I would've!' boasted Wright, puffing out his chest and slamming his fist on the table.

'Yeah – right!' said Torrey with a snigger. 'Shut the fuck up!'

'You shut the fuck up!' came Wright's swift response. 'You and your family can piss off for all I care!'

Then the arguing started again. Bob, who had continued to listen by his open bedroom door, found it quite amusing. However, Shane didn't. He heard every single word being said and, feeling hurt, as if he'd been shot in the chest by a Taliban bullet, stormed around the caravan enraged. Then, spotting his bike, he jumped upon it and rode as fast as he could to Grafton's, determined to show everyone he was no coward –

especially to little Bob.

Happening to look out the front window, Marian saw Shane leaving on his bike in a hurry. 'Where's Shane going?' she asked her husband as the others continued arguing. 'You don't think he's going to –'

'Looks like it,' replied Joe, already knowing what she was about to say. 'He's certainly heading towards Grafton's.'

'He must be mad – he's asking for trouble if he goes back there!' interjected Lewis, overhearing their conversation.

'Oh! Stop him, Joe! He's gonna get himself badly hurt or killed, even!'

Joe turned his head towards her. 'Even if I tried to stop him, Marian, I don't think it would do much good. He's got a sore itch that needs scratching!'

Marian looked worried.

'Besides,' continued Joe, 'we don't know he's going there. He missed his dinner, didn't he?' Marian nodded, looking slightly less worried. '... So maybe he's just off to town to get something from the chippie instead.'

'Perhaps you're right,' she said, unconvinced – which, truth be told, neither was he.

CHAPTER ELEVEN

Darkness had closed in by the time Shane reached Grafton's. The general store and café lights were out, and apart from a gaudy red neon sign hanging up outside the bar entrance, which simply read, 'BAR', and subdued lighting from within, the whole area was ... Well ... dark! The perfect setting to commit murder!

His assumption was correct: the white Toyota Hilux pickup truck belonging to one of the bullies was still outside – exactly where it had been earlier – and he recognised at least one of the voices bellowing above the sound of a Phil Collins track playing in the background. 'Red', he recalled the loudmouth's name to be.

Even though Shane felt like it, he didn't want to kill the uncouth brute who had first confronted him and tried to humiliate him earlier at the bar. Or any of his hyena-impersonating chums that egged him on. He did, however, wish to teach them all a hard lesson so they would never do it again.

Still seething, Shane jumped off his bike, letting it fall to the ground a short distance from the bar, unconcerned whether or not someone would steal it again. His attention was solely focused on the shabby entrance door.

Then the music stopped, and the neon light went out. Shane stopped in his tracks, allowing a few drunken locals to spill out of the bar and onto the warped and splintered decking before making their way home along the unlit dusty roadside. He watched them leave, waiting patiently in the shadows for the right moment to act out his revenge on the remaining baddies inside.

Then, moving swiftly towards the entrance, he suddenly stopped again. A black cat was sauntering along in front of him and about to cross his path. 'Shoo!' he said softly, allowing superstition to get the better of him. 'Shoo!' he repeated louder, but the cat still ignored him. He then made a sudden movement towards it, which this time sent the cat scurrying away in the other direction (which was most unlike Shane – to turn away a pussy).

Somewhat relieved, Shane finally approached the entrance, pausing only momentarily to take a deep breath. Then he burst in, allowing the heavy wooden door to crash fully open, causing the large windows to reverberate and startling everyone inside.

Red Marlin and Young Chris immediately swivelled on

their seats, shocked to see the cowboy standing between the doorway with his legs straddled widely apart, curling his upper lip and looking mean with his Stetson low on his brow.

'We're closed!' nervously uttered the barman, Will Atkey, before quickly disappearing below the bar. It was like a scene out of a Western movie!

Red staggered up first, garbling, 'Well, if it ain't Shane the fuckin' cowboy!' Then, grabbing an empty pint glass and smashing the rim against the table's edge, he spat, 'You've made a big mistake coming here tonight. I'm gonna cut choo up!'

Moving with lightning speed, Shane bravely headed straight for his armed foe, grabbing his weapon of choice as he did: a wooden chair. Coming at Shane, Red slashed at the air a couple of times. 'Go – get 'im!' yelled Young Chris in an excited, high-pitched voice. But by then, Shane was already swinging the chair from high above him towards the brute's head – too bad he wasn't wearing his hard hat this time! There was a sickening thudding sound as wood met bone. But unlike the movies, the chair remained intact, which Shane casually tossed aside as he watched the so-called hard man drop the glass in extreme pain, then stagger even more from side to side before his knees buckled, and he collapsed on the floor in a heap. But Shane wasn't done with him yet: removing a single black leather glove almost casually from his rear jeans pocket, he put it on his right hand, then interlaced his fingers to ensure it was on tight, clenching his fist a couple of times for good measure. Hearing a whimper from over on his right, Shane shot the stunned and petrified lad a glare. It looked as though he might have pissed himself, but it was hard to tell with all the spilt beer on the floor. 'Fuck off!' mouthed Shane, gesturing with his head towards the door. Scrambling to his feet, Young Chris didn't hesitate, running out the door faster than a speeding bullet – or chair! He wasn't as cocky now!

Turning his attention once again to his floored semi-conscious assailant, whose head injury had now caused blood to run down his chubby face, Shane straddled him and, grabbing his check shirt with his left hand and pulling him closer, said, 'The chair was for being rude to me earlier' – he clenched his gloved hand into a tight fist – 'and this is for damaging Mrs Starrett's picket fence and flowers!' Upon saying that, pulling his right arm back as far as it would go, he punched the lout square on the nose, breaking it instantly, then, without respite, continued until his face was a bruised and bloody mess.

When Shane had finished dishing out his punishment, he brought his head close to Red's ear and warned: 'Let this be a warning! If you or any of the other scumbags come looking for trouble, I'll be waiting! Cos I ain't goin' nowhere!' He then relaxed his left-hand grip, allowing the man's upper body to fall loosely back onto the floor, rose up, calmly readjusted his hat, and left.

Outside, Shane mounted his bike and rode back along the coast road to the Starrett's place. Once there, he opened the caravan door abruptly and, remaining in the doorway, to hushed silence, announced without emotion to the large group still there: 'Two of Fletcher's boys won't be troubling you again for a while!'

That succinctly said, Shane stepped back outside, closing the door sharply behind him, and headed around to the rear of the caravan.

A buzz of excitement immediately filled the caravan. Marian called out to Shane, but he didn't respond. 'Shane must've given those bastards a good seeing to!' said one man. 'I wonder which one's!' said another. 'Serves them right!' voiced Joe with glee. All talking over one another. Upon hearing Shane's distinctive voice, Bob sat bolt upright in bed. 'I knew he wasn't a coward!' he repeated to himself, pleased beyond measure.

Soon afterwards, an ambulance's flashing lights could be seen a mile down the road.

CHAPTER TWELVE

The following morning, candyfloss skies sweetened the bitterness of the stormy atmosphere the night before, and calm washed over Shane as he submerged himself beneath the blue during his regular early morning dip.

Then, after his refreshing swim, he continued his exercise, running along the water's edge towards Folkestone. Maybe he should continue running as far as Folkestone and get on a ferry to France, he told himself, which would be a bit weird, he acknowledged with the briefest of smiles, given that he was only wearing white jockeys! His troubling thoughts had quickly returned – he hardly slept a wink following his outrage at Grafton's, which hospitalised one of Fletcher's boys. He couldn't give a toss about the bully's well-being – he deserved it as far as Shane was concerned. He even doubted whether the likes of Fletcher would involve the police. What bothered him the most was not if, but when the nasty bastard would retaliate and cause further grief to the Starretts and their fellow Travellers. As regards himself, he cared far less! No, he couldn't abandon them now. Not after the kindness they had shown him. He would stay for as long as his hosts would have him, or until his misdemeanours caught up with him, and he was handcuffed and taken away by the authorities.

When Shane returned to the Starretts' premises, still only dressed in his jockeys and cowboy boots, the smell of sausage and bacon immediately filled his nostrils, making him feel hungry. Moving swiftly around the side of the caravan to get changed before filling his chops with grub, Marian almost threw herself at him as he turned the corner. She was wearing a sexy, short black satin kimono with nothing on beneath. *'Shane!'* she said, almost startling the poor guy. Pressing him up against the rear of the caravan, she asked, 'Are you all right?' He could smell alcohol on her breath. And then, to his pleasant surprise, her kimono suddenly flapped open, exposing her enormous boobs. Her nipples were hard, and she had a lustful look in her eyes. 'I was worried about you!'

'I'm fine,' he hurriedly answered. 'I'd better get dressed for breakfast.' He tried to move forward, but she pressed her palm against his manly hairy chest even firmer.

'You look fine as you are to me!' she commented, staring down at the outline of his cock through his tight, wet underwear.

'Where's Joe and Bob?' he nervously asked.

'Oh, Joe took Bob fishing early this morning.' She answered with a glint in her eye. 'So, it's just you and me here!'

Fuck! he thought, panicking slightly. Shane started to speak, but the sex freak put a finger to her lips and said, 'Shhh!' The next thing he knew was her other hand slipping down his jocks and grabbing his manhood. 'You seem stressed – let me help you feel more relaxed!'

I'm not surprised, he thought, *with your hand down my fuckin' pants! What if Joe comes back!*

Shane could feel his cock getting stiffer as his knob rubbed against the 70% nylon/30% cotton material as she began rapidly wanking him off. He let his head rest against the caravan and closed his eyes, feeling a rush of excitement and dread. Then he felt his jocks being sharply pulled southward to his knees. Opening his eyes momentarily, he saw the temptress now squatting with her mouth wide open, ready to devour him. Her legs were wide apart, revealing her jet-black, hairy snatch. *She dyes her hair blonde!* he immediately thought.

'Stop!' he pathetically called out. But it was too late: Marian took his whole eight inches into her mouth and down her throat and began moving her head rapidly back and forth. The term 'maneater' sprang to mind – quite literally! 'STOP!'

'But I thought you were enjoying it?' she garbled as

she pulled his throbbing, meaty shaft from out of her mouth.

Disappointed, she let go of it, then stood up and covered herself up.

'It's not that I don't like it,' he sorrowfully explained as he quickly pulled his Jockeys up, unable to cover his knob, which glistened with her saliva over the top of the waistband. 'It's out of respect for Joe.'

Marian laughed. 'Joe doesn't give a fuck!' she cynically stated. 'He's too busy fucking Will Atkey's young whore of a wife, Melisa, and any other foolish woman that'll fall for his Irish charm and part her legs for him!' Then, scowling, 'She's a sex maniac!'

I know someone else like that, thought Shane. Then, before Shane could speak:

'Don't worry about it, darling,' she said, clearly miffed, 'Your breakfast is in the pan.' Suddenly, she let out an enormous scream. 'SHIT! I must've left the gas on!' Dashing up the rear steps and entering the caravan, Marian and Shane could immediately smell burning and saw flames leaping out of the pan, almost as high as the ceiling!

Acting quickly, Shane turned off the gas. Then, grabbed a large tea towel and, after soaking it in cold water from the tap, threw it over the pan to extinguish the flames.

'Oh, sweet mother of Jesus!' said Marian, coughing

and spluttering as she speedily opened all the windows to let out the acrid smoke. 'I could've burnt the place down!'

Looking up, the ceiling above the stove was black with soot. 'I told Joe to get some bleedin' new batteries for the smoke alarm!' bemoaned his wife with a shake of the head. Greatly relieved, however, that a black ceiling was all she had to worry about! Thanks to Shane.

CHAPTER THIRTEEN

'What am I gonna do!' asked Marian, looking at the blackened ceiling in despair. 'Joe's not gonna be very happy.'

'Do you have any white paint?' asked Shane, quickly coming up with a solution. By now his cock had shrivelled back into his pants.

Marian nodded. 'I think so.'

'Well, you go and fetch it, and I'll have it painted before Joe returns,' he told her. 'He'll be none the wiser!'

'Oh, thank you, Shane!' she said, before rushing off to look for the paint. 'You're my hero!'

Shane just smiled and shook his head in amusement. Then, feeling mighty hungry, reached into the frying pan and picked up a charred, fat, juicy sausage. He was about to bite halfway into it before quickly changing his mind when he suddenly got a flashback of Marian performing deep-throat on him.

'There!' said Shane, after applying the last lick of paint

to the ceiling. 'You can hardly notice the difference!' Except that the rest of the ceiling now looked dirty by comparison.

During the time Shane spent painting, while balancing precariously on a slightly wobbly wooden stool, Marian and he spoke at greater length than usual, and he was more candid about his life than ever before:

'I heard the ambulance last night ...' said Marian, now more collected. There was a pause. Then she spoke again. 'Was he badly hurt?'

Shane looked at her from his lofty position, simply answering, 'He'll live.'

'Well, the asshole deserved it – coming here – ruining my geraniums!' Then after a beat. 'I doubt very much, though, that'll be the end of it. Fletcher's not the sort that gives in easily. And he's got plenty more undesirables in his pocket that can take Red's place!'

'Yeah, well, we'll cross that bridge when we come to it,' Shane remarked as he continued brushing.

'So, you're not leaving us then?' she asked, pleased to hear.

Shane shook his head. 'No – what made you think that?'

'Well, it's just that I thought –'

Shane didn't wait for her explanation. 'Look. I'll stay for as long as you need my help.'

'We are glad to have you here, Shane!' A pause. 'I hear

you call out in the night sometimes …' He listened without comment at first. 'Sounds like you're having terrible nightmares!'

Shane dismissed it with a titter at first. He was never one to talk about himself, let alone his embattled and troubled mind. He was likely suffering from PTSD but had never had a diagnosis. Like many war veterans, he just got on with life and battled through it.

'… Were you in the armed forces?' Marian asked him directly. He shot her a certain look, and she could tell he felt uncomfortable talking about it.

But then, after a moment, he nodded, saying, 'Yeah. I fought in Afghanistan.'

That would explain it, she thought, *probably flashbacks.* She opened her mouth to say as much, but to her surprise, the usually taciturn man continued.

'War is a grim business!'

'Oh, my husband thought you were a soldier. He noticed the tattoo on your forearm.'

'Evidence of a drunken night out on leave with the lads!' he replied lightly as he applied more paint to the ceiling. Then, changing the subject, 'Any chance of a cuppa tea?'

'Sure!' she answered, getting the message. Whatever it was keeping Shane awake at night, she could tell he preferred to keep buried, so she didn't persist in questioning him about it anymore and went and put the kettle on. Once she'd brought him a mug of tea, though, she did ask him about his love life:

'So, how come a handsome man like you isn't married with children by now, then?'

He smiled. 'Well, I guess 'cos I'm not the kinda fella to settle down.'

'But you must have had plenty of girlfriends over the –'

'No – not really,' he replied with a slight shake of the head, pausing from his work momentarily. 'I mean, I've had a few relationships, but they never seem to last very long.'

'That surprises me,' she told him. 'Well, I'd better get dressed' – she casually flashed her boobs again as she adjusted her kimono – 'and let you get on!' Then, giving him a lingering 'come to bed with me' look, she turned on her heels, and that's where she headed.

Resisting the urge to succumb to her temptations and join her, he merely said, 'See ya soon!'

Feeling somewhat disappointed but trying not to show it, it wasn't long before the temptress returned, dressed in a provocative, tight-fitting, flowery summer dress – like Fletcher, she wasn't one to give in easily either.

'Nearly done!' he called out. Then, turning toward Marian, she noticed his face splattered with white paint, making her chuckle.

Just then, the usual racket from the building site

started.

'Oh, why the hell do they have to start work so bloody early for!' she moaned. 'I'm sure it's just to piss me off!'

While Shane and Marian were busy chatting in the caravan, so were Fletcher and his boys, inside the building site's Portakabin office – and Fletcher was not a happy bunny!

'... Why the fuck, Chris, did you scarper when Red was being pummelled on the ground by that tosser cowboy?' demanded Fletcher, looking directly at him. Young Chris, Curly, and Morgan sat on tatty grey plastic chairs on both sides, while Fletcher sat on his high-backed, black leather-bound chair, behind his large 'I'm the big fucking cheese' desk. Red was still in the hospital undergoing treatment.

'Well ... well ... I-I went to get help!' answered Young Chris nervously.

'Shit-scared, more like!' jibbed Curly with a snigger.

'Be quiet!' snapped Fletcher. Then, after a moment, 'Sounds like this cowboy fella – what's his name?'

'Shane,' informed his right-hand man, Morgan.

'Sounds like he knows how to throw a punch!' continued the boss.

'Leave it to me, Mr Fletcher – I'll sort him out!' said Morgan, clenching his fist unconsciously.

Fletcher slowly nodded. 'Good. The sooner we get shot of him, the better.' Then, after a beat, he added,

'You'd better take these two' – he gestured with his head towards Young Chris and Curly – 'and maybe one or two others to make sure he doesn't cause us any more problems!'

'Yes, boss!' said Morgan, quickly followed by the other two. His boys all feared him: it was no secret that Fletcher was connected.

CHAPTER FOURTEEN

Now fully dressed, Shane decided that a trip to the café would be his best chance of having a hearty breakfast. By now, he was ready to eat a horse (not one of Marian's)! So, off he went – this time on foot.

On his way, he saw two boys farther along arguing about something. One was wearing a cowboy outfit, whom, at first, he assumed was Bob. The cheap, Chinese-made costume certainly looked like the one he had bought the lad the day before. But when he got closer, he realised that it was Bob's so-called friend, Ollie Johnson, wearing it, and he could hear Bob telling him to take it off and give it back to him, saying repeatedly, 'It's mine!'

'I *found* it!' argued Ollie. 'So now it's *mine!* Finders keepers, losers weepers!'

The argument was becoming increasingly heated, and the two boys began pushing and shoving one another, which quickly turned into a fistfight. And from what Shane could tell, now only a few metres away, Bob was coming off much worse – taking several blows to his face and midriff.

'STOP!' shouted Shane. But before he could reach them and put a stop to it, Bob was curled up on the dusty ground in agony, winded from the last punch, and Ollie had begun kicking him.

Standing between them and holding his arms out to prevent Ollie from continuing, Shane again shouted, 'STOP I SAID!'

'HE STARTED IT!' Ollie shouted back as he backed away slightly in a huff.

'Yeah, well, I'm finishing it! Now go back to your parents or else!'

He then called Shane a wanker and ran off.

Once the lippy boy left, Shane crouched beside Bob and helped him sit up. He was still clutching his abdomen, his left cheek looked puffy, and his lip was bleeding slightly.

'He stole my cowboy outfit!' claimed Bob, still annoyed.

'Don't worry – I'll buy you another one!' said Shane as he helped the injured lad to his feet.

'You will?' replied Bob with a growing smile, almost forgetting about the pain.

'Sure!' Shane reassured him before asking, 'Where's your father? I thought you'd gone fishing together.'

'We did. But after dropping me off at my friend Ollie's,

he told me he needed to visit Aunt Melisa because she's poorly – she's from Hong Kong!'

'Oh, really?' replied Shane, slightly amused.

'Yeah!'

'Well, Bob. I was on my way to Grafton's to get a bite to eat,' began Shane. 'Do you think you can manage to walk home by yourself?' Bob nodded. 'Your Mum's at home – she'll sort you out!' It wasn't very far, and Shane could see that Bob wasn't badly hurt.

'If you see any more of Fletcher's gang, are you gonna beat them up, Shane?' said the boy excitedly. 'Like you did with those two baddies last night?'

Shane looked serious for a moment, then smiled. 'No, Bobby-boy. I don't think that'll be necessary anymore. I doubt that they'll be bothering us again!' Even as he said those assuring words, Shane knew that that was highly unlikely! Still, he didn't want to worry the lad.

'Take care now!' said Shane. 'And when I return, I'll start giving you self-defence lessons!'

'Really, Mr Shane?' exuberantly expressed Bob.

Shane nodded with a warm smile. 'Really!'

'Okay! Bye, Shane!' The boy waved goodbye, chuffed that his hero would teach him how to fight, and left. Shane waved back, then watched him for a short while to make sure he was okay.

It was around nine o'clock, and as Shane entered the café, the smell of cooked food filled his nostrils again. It was reasonably busy still – mostly with workmen tucking into a Full English Breakfast and drinking mugs of Builder's Tea, with the teabag tab still hanging out – but Shane found a small table for two and sat down.

Quickly scanning the room, he didn't recognise any of the troublemakers. But he sat with his back to the wall, facing outward, like he always liked to, in case trouble should come looking.

Shane hadn't been sitting down that long when the owner breezed over. At first, Shane thought he would perhaps complain about last night and tell him to leave. But no, it was the complete opposite: instead, he shook Shane's hand, full of smiles, telling him that it was about time somebody stood up to Fletcher and his boys. And he even offered Shane a fully cooked breakfast without charge! 'It used to be peaceful and friendly around here before that darn developer showed up!' moaned Sam Grafton quietly, with a slight shake of the head.

Somewhat relieved that the owner wasn't involving the police or charging him for any damages there may have been, Shane began to relax and enjoy his sumptuous breakfast. He noticed the chef coming hastily from the kitchen, sweating heavily, with large, greasy stainless steel containers of steaming hot food to replenish the breakfast buffet bar. He was a bald, squatty fella in his late thirties. And serving the food was a young, attractive teenage girl with dark hair tied back in a ponytail – who, as Shane later found out, was the owner's rebellious seventeen-year-old daughter.

The 'Ugly Sisters' (the nickname Shane gave them) were also there, sitting at the same table as yesterday, wearing the same outfits and drinking strawberry milkshakes again. *Maybe they hadn't left,* he mused with a wry smile.

One of them kept giving him the eye. Finding it difficult to ignore, Shane looked across and offered her a faint smile, only to find the twenty-something woman prising her chubby legs wide apart. He watched in mild disbelief and strange fascination as her sweaty skin resisted such action and clung together for as long as possible. Then, reaching below the table, she swiftly pulled the knicker elastic to one side, exposing her Hollywood-look pussy. He quickly diverted his gaze back to his plate, thinking what the fuck just happened – glad he hadn't chosen the kippers for breakfast. 'If she wrapped her legs around ya, you'd never escape!' he said to himself, wincing and shuddering slightly.

She and her look-alike's attention was then diverted suddenly: a shifty-looking, short, skinny young man with long, unkempt jet-black hair, wearing a black hoodie and carrying one of those poncy man-bags over his shoulder had just walked in and headed straight towards the two young women. He had a cigarette behind one ear and walked with a kind of cocky swagger. The lad – nicknamed 'Spliffy' – then pulled up a chair and sat down between them. Opening his mouth to speak, Shane immediately recognised a Mancunian accent. He spoke very rapidly, and it was hard to understand what the bleedin' hell he was saying.

Daring to glance over again, lest he see her snatch one more time, he noticed the geezer secretly handing the flasher a small packet under the table. Drugs, Shane immediately thought. He tried to ignore their underhanded (or under-the-table!) antics and continued eating his breakfast. But, to his annoyance and disgust, he was quickly distracted again by the slurping sounds coming from that direction. And, this time, it wasn't the 'Ugly Sisters' sucking the dregs of their milkshakes through a straw: it was the pair of them snogging the head off of the drug dealer while he had his hand up one of their skirts. Shane shuddered again and pushed his plate forward on the table. It put him right off!

Shortly afterwards, the big shot (or little shot) swaggered his way back out of the premises. Pretending not to notice while drinking his mug of tea, Shane then saw him cross the road and step onto the pebble beach. There, the scumbag was soon joined by a young lady who looked the spitting image of the waitress. He thought he must be seeing things at first. Until he cranked his neck around and noticed she was no longer behind the buffet bar. She must've sneaked out the back, he thought. Quickly looking out the window again, he spotted them handing each other something before she turned and hurried back towards the café. Was she also buying drugs, then crossed his mind? It looked suspiciously like it. *I bet her father wouldn't be too pleased!*

'Don't get involved,' he told himself. 'You're in enough shit as it is!' Then, taking one last sip of tea, he got up, gestured his thanks to the owner, and strode outside. The time for contemplation was over. He'd decided he couldn't let this pass, and although he certainly didn't want the cops' big noses snooping around, he would have a strong word in the detestable lad's ear instead – and rough him up a little if need be. Then, suddenly remembering he promised to buy little Bob another cowboy outfit, he returned and purchased the last one.

When he did finally leave, the drug dealer was gone.

Meanwhile, back at the caravan, Joe Starrett had just returned home.

'What's that smell?!' he immediately asked his wife upon entering, sniffing around.

She was sitting down, puffing away at a cigarette with a half-drunk mug of coffee in front of her. 'What smell?' she replied through a cloud of smoke.

'It smells like paint to me!'

'I don't know what you're talking about,' she told him,

hoping he didn't look up. 'Anyway – how was fishing? Did you catch anything? Crabs or herpes?' He didn't fool his wife for one minute – and 'going fishing' had become a euphemism for casting his rod into far murkier waters than the sea – especially if Melisa Atkey's husband found out. He may be cowardly most of the time, but he gets very jealous and protective when it comes to his Asian wife. Marian didn't wait for a response, adding cuttingly, 'Anyway, with your small bait, I'm surprised you can catch anything!'

Joe feigned a blank look, then quickly changed the subject, saying, 'I need a shower!' and strutted off in the direction of the bathroom.

Bob was fine once his mum had patched him up. He was out back, happily tending to the livestock. But that wasn't the only thing little Bob was doing: while Shane wasn't around, he decided to have a nose around inside the camper van, which he found, on this occasion, unlocked.

Little Bob couldn't believe his eyes when he unzipped Shane's tatty-old rucksack and discovered what was inside: wrapped carefully in a grubby white towel was a toy gun. Only it wasn't a toy! It was an authentic Glock 17 (the British Special Forces standard issue sidearm). And the lethal weapon was loaded!

The excited, wide-eyed kid immediately picked it up and took it outside to play with – aiming it at anything that moved and pretending to shoot. Lord only knows what would have happened if he had pressed the trigger fully! That's when Shane suddenly returned.

'WHOA! WHOA!' screamed Shane as he turned the corner and saw Bob pointing his gun directly at him. 'Put the gun down, Bob! There's a good lad!'

Shane's raised voice startled little Bob, who promptly lowered the gun to the ground.

Realising he'd frightened and upset the lad, Shane softened his tone a little, saying, 'Here – this gun is for you!' He hurriedly handed Bob the cowboy outfit package containing the holstered toy gun, then bent down and picked up the real one, mightily relieved it hadn't discharged. Immediately storing the weapon away, he asked, 'What were you doing looking inside my rucksack?'

The nervous boy looked up at him and could only mutter: 'Erm – well ... the van door was open and ...'

'Never mind,' said Shane, realising he was partly to blame. 'But in the future, don't go snooping among my things! Do you hear?'

Bob nodded. There was a pause before he asked: 'Is yours a real gun? It sure felt heavy!'

Shane shook his head, 'No – of course not!'

Then smiling, Bob said, 'Thank you for my cowboy outfit, Mr Shane!' and quickly headed inside to try it on.

CHAPTER FIFTEEN

Two days later, parked along the top road, not far from the new luxury development site entrance, Fletcher waited alone in his Range Rover. A glance at his Rolex read: 8:35 am. Getting ever more impatient, he lowered his window and lit a Cuban cigar to help calm his nerves. He'd only taken two puffs when a sparkling silver Toyota Corolla pulled up behind him.

Sitting anxiously behind the wheel and dressed in plain clothes to conceal his identity was Chief Superintendent Bob Tomkins – a close associate of Fletcher's and fellow Mason.

Quickly stubbing his cigar out, Fletcher got out of the car, muttering to himself, 'About bloody time!' and walked over to the Corolla, not best pleased.

The superintendent lowered his window to be greeted with, 'You're late!' Then, adopting a friendlier tone, Fletcher remarked, 'New car?'

'Yeah!' replied Tomkins.

'Nice!' expressed Fletcher, hiding his insincerity well.

'Listen, Bob. I've got a problem. There's a stranger in town who is staying at the Starrett's place. He had a run-in with one of my boys the other day. Red Marlin! Beat him half to death, he did.'

The superintendent acted surprised. 'Did Red report it to the police?'

'Nah – don't be daft! What good would that do?'

The copper chuckled.

'Now I'm not saying that Red didn't goad the fella to begin with – you know what he can be like once he's had a drink – but this bum's trouble, do ya hear me?' The copper nodded. 'It's hard enough to get rid of the Gypo's as it is, let alone without him interfering in support of them!'

'Do you know his name?'

'Shaun somebody or other.'

'Well, what's he look like?'

'He dresses like a cowboy! He's a fuckin' weirdo –'

'So, what do you want me to do about it?' interjected the copper, having got the picture. 'Unless someone reports a crime, there's very little I can do.'

'Do a bit of sniffing around. Find out if he has a criminal record or if he's a wanted man. After all, that's what you cops are supposed to be good at, aren't cha?'

'No problem – leave it with me, Luke.' There was a pause. 'Okay, well, if that'll be all ...'

'Well, there is just one more thing.'

His associate looked at him as if to say, ‘Go on.’

‘... I’m off on holiday today for a couple of weeks with the Mrs.’

‘Lucky you!’

‘Yeah, well, listen. I’ve told the boys I want the piece of shit gone by the time I get back!’ Fletcher then leaned closer to his associate, resting his elbow against the window frame and locking eyes. ‘And by whatever means necessary, if you get my drift.’ The slightly uneasy cop nodded. ‘I trust I’ll have your full support, Bob!’

'Of course – but try not to make it too messy, or that might prove more challenging.’

Fletcher just grinned. Then, reaching into his inner jacket pocket, he pulled out a thick, sealed envelope and handed it over to the bent cop. He then tapped the roof twice as if to suggest, almost dismissively, that he was done with him. The engine started. Then, as an afterthought, the local gangster said, ‘See you on the golf course when I return, shall I?’

‘Yeah, sure!’ the superintendent replied, then sharply drove off.

CHAPTER SIXTEEN

Two weeks rolled by without incident, and all seemed strangely calm and peaceful among the town's folk living along the New Romney shoreline. Shane continued working for the Starretts – mostly helping Joe build driveways, fixing roofs, and doing the odd spot of window cleaning (which usually ended up dirtier than when he started). He also managed to avoid Marian's lustful advances! Marian kept busy tending to her garden and cooking. And Bob had since made friends with Ollie again and did what most boys his age do during the school summer holidays: skylark about. During that time, Shane also gave Bob self-defence lessons, much to Marian's angst, who worried about her boy getting hurt. But as Shane pointed out, it would help prevent him from getting hurt! And as for Fletcher and his boys, word had it, he was staying at his luxury villa in sunny Spain while they continued working on the building site. And, miraculously, appeared to keep themselves out of trouble – at least for the time being!

Was it the lull before the storm? Or had it already passed, and the developer would now leave the Travellers be? Shane and his beleaguered new friends could only but wonder – hope. Whatever the case, for now, they intended to enjoy the beautiful, calm weather and tranquillity while it lasted.

The truth was that Fletcher's 'boys' had merely been waiting for the right moment to set upon Shane and send him on his way – in a body bag if need be – without too many eyes witnessing! Due to a busy work schedule, Shane had rarely been around, let alone visited Grafton's. But it would only be a matter of time before that day came.

Well, as it turned out, that day was today:

'Say, Shane,' began Joe chirpily inside the caravan Saturday morning. 'How would you like to come to Grafton's with a few other families and us and celebrate Lew Johnson's birthday today?'

'Well ...' replied Shane with a slight reluctance.

'Oh – come on, Shane! It'll do you good to let your hair down a bit!' said Marian, trying to persuade him. 'I don't think Fletcher and his boys are gonna give us any bother again.'

'I think you must've frightened them off!' added Joe with a chuckle. 'You've worked hard and deserve it. Come on! What d'ya say?'

'Well, okay then!' Shane agreed, smiling back.

Bob was, of course, overjoyed upon hearing that Shane was coming, too.

So, dressed in their finest, Joe, Marian, Bob, and Shane headed to Grafton's on foot, joined by other Travellers' families along the way. It was a beautiful day, and everyone was in good spirits – well, almost everyone.

'Oh, why couldn't we have taken one of the bleedin' vehicles or at least the sulky!' moaned Marian, struggling to walk in her six-inch heels.

'Because the car still needs fixing, the truck is jampacked full of tools, and as for the sulky, may I remind you what happened the last time we rode that death trap!'

'What's a *sulky?'* asked Shane, completely baffled.

'A horse and cart,' answered Bob with a chuckle.

'Look, it's a lovely day! Why can't you just enjoy yourself, Marian, instead of moaning,' said her husband, slightly up ahead.

'You try wearing high heels, ya bastard!' returned his miffed wife. *'Wait up!'*

Shane and Bob looked at each other and grinned.

Watching from one of the newly-built luxury property balconies were Morgan, Curly, Young Chris, and Red Marlin, who still had a nasal splint over his nose.

'Looks like they're all heading for Grafton's!' said Young Chris with unbridled excitement. 'And that cowboy fella is among 'em!' It was hard to miss his wide-brimmed hat!

'We need to act now!' said Red, keen to exact his revenge on Shane. 'The boss'll be back from Spain this evening!'

'Don't worry, you'll get your revenge today!' replied Morgan, straight talking as he looked through his binoculars. 'Look at those slags, all tarted up!'

'I'd shag the Starrett lady!' commented Young Chris.

The others laughed.

'She's old enough to be your mother!' said Morgan, pulling a face.

'Grandmother, more like!' joked Red to more laughter.

There was a pause while the laughter subsided, then in a more serious vein, Morgan said: 'We'll wait for the cowboy to enter, then we'll catch him by surprise.'

'Won't there be too many witnesses?!' said Curly with a worrisome look.

'Now that most of the tourists have left,' answered Morgan, 'I don't think we need to concern ourselves about that. And as for the locals and that trash down there.' He nodded in the Travellers' direction. 'They will be too chicken-shit scared to do anything about it!' He clenched his fists so tightly that his bones cracked.

When the large, noisy crowd arrived at Grafton's around midday – slightly sweatier than when they set off – they found they had the place virtually to themselves. Granted, a few small pockets of locals immediately got up and left upon the Traveller's arrival. The 'Ugly Sisters' remained, though, and also that old bloke who gazes out the window a lot. They were taunting again as usual: 'He's staring at your boobs!' one said to the other. 'Fuck off, you old pervert!' nastily said the other, despite his pleas to leave him alone.

'It's Joe Starrett's round!' called out one of the Travellers as they piled into the premises.

'No, it bloody isn't!' replied Joe, quick off the mark.

There was much laughter: when it came to buying drinks, Joe wasn't known for his generosity.

'I'll get the first round!' insisted the Birthday Boy, celebrating his sixty-ninth birthday. 'You lot can squabble about who's gonna buy the rounds after that!'

'Hey, Torrey!' called Earnie Wright. 'You look worn out!'

'I'm not surprised with all the kids he's got!' joked Joe, causing much laughter.

'Fuck off, the lot yis!' replied Torrey in good spirit, panting a little still in his rush to get there.

The owner, Sam Grafton, then came rushing over. 'I'm afraid the bar doesn't open until twelve!'

Quickly looking at their fake Rolexes and mobile phones, a few of the Travellers noticed it was 11:55 am. The barman, Will Atkey, peered around the corner, looking forlorn.

'Oh, *what?'* expressed Marian, dying for a double gin and tonic, followed by a few other shouts of disapproval from the others.

'Can't you make an exception!' cried Earnie Wright, still outside the entrance door, trying to get in. 'It's Lew's birthday!'

'I'm sorry – I'm afraid I can't!' said the owner, shaking his head insistently. 'But the café and shop are open.' He then added sternly, 'And no stealing!'

'What does he take us for?' said Marian to her husband, who seemed more interested in getting to the fishing tackle section than listening to her.

And, to the sound of moans, groans, and tutting, the Travellers begrudgingly sat in the café or mooched around the shop.

Happening to be standing right next to the owner, Shane began chatting with him. He'd noticed that his daughter was not around, and another girl of a similar age was serving customers in the café.

'Where's your daughter today then?' asked Shane, making polite conversation.

Mr Grafton looked at him as if gravely concerned. 'Jane is resting at home. A few days ago, I discovered her collapsed on her bedroom floor next to a pile of vomit after taking an amphetamine overdose!' He started to tear up and appeared unsteady on his feet. 'I had no idea she was taking it. Ever since her mum died, looking after her as well as trying to run the business has been very hard.'

Shane slowly nodded, putting his hand on Joe's shoulder for support.

'Thank goodness the ambulance came in time! She could've died!' continued the owner. He then pulled an angry face. 'I wish I could get my hands on the culprit who supplied her with drugs!'

Shane had a good idea who that despicable low-life was and immediately wished he'd have acted sooner when he saw the pair together. Then, perhaps the trauma it had caused wouldn't have happened in the first place!

'That's shocking to hear,' expressed Shane. 'Well, I wish her a speedy recovery!'

Just then, the noise erupted, and there was a sudden surge towards the bar. A stampede almost!

The bar suddenly became swamped, and poor ol' Will Atkey struggled to cope until his lazy wife came hurrying from the direction of the storeroom, looking very dishevelled to the last few bars of 5, 6, 7, 8 by Steps.

'Where've you been!' Will asked her, not at all happy.

'I was helping the chef stick his toad in the hole,' she answered coyly, blushing slightly.

I bet you were, Will thought angrily.

She'd only served a couple of customers when she suddenly announced in her broken English, 'I must dash!

I've got an appointment at the nail polish bar!' Saying that, she quickly removed her pinny, tossed it aside, and promptly left. The real reason she left in such a hurry, however, was that she'd just seen Joe Starrett's wife enter the bar and didn't want a confrontation.

Shane sat in the café drinking black coffee and showing the kids card tricks. He hadn't touched a drop of alcohol since leaving the military. Overhearing the gobby 'Ugly Sisters' being rude to the old man again, this time, he decided to confront the cruel pair. He noticed the Paras emblem sewn to the outer breast pocket of the meek man's crumpled, shabby old blazer. He was a war veteran like him. 'Leave him be,' he firmly told them. 'You should respect your elders!'

Now, whether it was his tone of voice, the way he looked at them, or both, the pair immediately rose to their feet in unison and, after telling him to fuck off, they fucked off instead. The old man cracked a rare smile and acknowledged his thanks with a nod towards the mysterious stranger.

Once the Travellers had bought drinks, many poured themselves back into the café, where there was more space, and ordered food. Shane didn't care much for crowds, promptly deciding to manoeuvre himself in the opposite direction towards the bar.

He had only just approached the bar when the few remaining patrons promptly got up and left for some strange reason. He wanted to buy a Coke – more caffeine to keep himself awake after a restless night listening to Marian's loud and prolonged orgasms – but the bartender also suddenly decided to disappear.

Leaning across the bar with his back to the door while another corny up-tempo track played loudly through the tinny sound system, Shane hadn't heard its hinges creak open, nor had he heard the footsteps of the six troublesome-looking figures who entered.

Then, Shane heard Bob's troubled voice trying to warn him to leave. Bob had spotted Fletcher's boys gathering outside and came into the bar to warn him. But it was too late by then: the thugs were already inside and spread out. They were snarling at him like wild dogs baying for his blood.

'Go to your mother, Bob,' Shane calmly said to the anxious boy after casually placing his hat on the bar and turning around.

'Come quickly, Shane!' begged Bob, sensing the imminent threat.

'You wouldn't want me to run like a coward now, would you?' said Shane, with one eye on Bob and the other on his foes.

'But Shane – there are too many of them!' replied Bob, frightened for his hero.

'Do as I say!'

Bob reluctantly turned and left.

'We warned you to leave, cowboy!' said the big, fat, ugly bastard, Morgan, standing only two metres before him. 'Now we're gonna make sure of it!'

At that moment, Shane saw Red Marlin step out from behind Morgan's huge frame, wielding a baseball bat, determined to get his revenge!

'He's a handsome fella, ain't he?' said Red with a smirk as he smacked the side of the bat against his sweaty, chubby palm a couple of times. 'Too bad I'm gonna rearrange his face!' This caused a few titters among Fletcher's boys.

'Get 'Im!' barked Morgan.

Then all hell broke loose! Red came at Shane first, yelling and swinging his bat towards his head as if it were a baseball. Anticipating, Shane immediately crouched, feeling only the breeze it created as it whizzed above his head. Then, before Red could make another attempt at cracking his skull open, he rose with lightning speed and punched his assailant right on the nose, instantly fracturing it again, before swiftly disarming him as easily as taking a toy from a small child. And with the bat now in his possession, he wasted no time putting it to use. While Red remained hunched over in a compromised position with blood pouring from his nostrils, the fearless protagonist whacked the back of his flabby neck, causing him to collapse instantly to the ground in immense pain. 'Some people never learn!' muttered Shane. But the brawl had only just begun, and there were still five more to contend with.

Morgan quickly stepped forward, waving his huge fists in the air and almost tripping over Red as he did, while Young Chris and Curly came at him from the sides. Raising the bat, Shane began swinging it from side to side, causing his would-be attackers to back off slightly. Then, a chair, whizzing through the air, struck Shane, sending him reeling backwards against the bar. Feeling slightly dazed, he dropped the bat as he tried to cling to the edge of the bar, only just about managing to stay on his feet.

Quickly taking advantage, Morgan took a swipe at Shane's head, which he dodged, immediately bringing his knee up and thrusting his steel-capped boot against the beast's abdomen, sending him reeling backwards and almost back out the door.

Meanwhile, Red had slid out of the way and was now leaning against a wall, nursing his nose. Through blurry eyes, he watched as the cowboy effortlessly dealt with Curly and Young Chris. First was Young Chris, who had attempted to pick up the baseball bat before Shane quickly stepped on it, preventing him from doing so. A sharp upward thrust of his knee under the lad's chin took care of him for the moment.

Coming at Shane from the other side, 'Have some of this, you cunt!' screamed Curly, throwing a hopeless punch and missing completely. Using his shoulder, Shane powerfully nudged him against the chest, sending his lanky body crashing against a nearby table and chairs. Then two others Shane didn't recognise came bounding towards him, throwing fists and abuse. Most of the strikes he swerved or blocked, but one fist caught him on the kisser, instantly causing his lip to bleed. But these two losers were no match for him, and for every punch they landed, his blows made contact far more!

Not wanting to miss the action, little Bob had since crawled back into the bar and hid under a table, cheering at every punch and kick his hero made and cringing at the rare occasion he got hit.

Bloodied and bruised, one of the attackers gave up and hobbled straight out the door. 'Come back here, you coward!' shouted Morgan, heading in the opposite direction towards Shane, who, as well as the guy he was continuing to fight, also had Curly and Young Chris to contend with again.

Swiftly moving away from the bar as empty glasses and chairs hurtled his way, pushing Curly aside again, Shane jumped onto a table and, using it like a springboard, threw himself at Morgan, catching his throat in the crook of his arm and forcing him on his back with a loud thud like one sees in a WWE smackdown.

Despite the music blaring out, the increasingly loud noise in the bar had carried, arousing the attention of the Travellers in the café and causing the hapless owner to hurry into the bar, shouting angrily, 'Whatever you break, you pay for!'

'What's that racket?!' questioned Marian, smoking outside the café with her man.

'Kylie Minogue!' answered Joe.

'No! *Listen!* It sounds like a fight!'

'I think you might be right!' he said, brushing past her and back into the café. She quickly followed behind.

Inside the café, fellow Travellers were advising each other not to get involved. 'It will only bring more trouble!' warned one. 'Let's go!' said another worried soul as genuine fear quickly spread among them.

Hurrying to the bar, Joe removed his tweed jacket, tossed it aside, and rolled up his shirt sleeves.

'Where are you going?!' said his wife, trying to keep up with him, deeply concerned. 'Don't go in there, Joe. You'll get hurt!'

'I can't leave Shane to fight alone, Marian!'

'Let me call the police and let them deal with it – it's too dangerous!' Marian grabbed his arm to stop him, but he snatched it away.

Raging, with his fists clenched, the big man burst into the bar area.

While most of the Travellers began to exit, fearing for

their family's safety, Marian and a couple of others remained within the shop, watching on with trepidation.

Joe entered the fray just in the nick of time because, despite Shane's best efforts to fight off the pack, it wasn't long before he'd become overwhelmed and was now being punched repeatedly in the face and stomach by Morgan while Curly and Young Chris held his arms!

'GET OFF HIM!' screamed Joe as he picked up one of the few upright chairs and planted it upon Morgan's bonce.

Unfortunately, it seemed to have little or no effect on the brute, who continued to take great satisfaction in giving Shane a beating. It worked the fourth time, though, causing him to collapse to the floor.

Somehow finding the strength, Shane swung the two cretins either side of him together with force, painfully causing them to clash heads and fall on top of Morgan in a heap. Then, a few well-placed kicks with his steel-capped boots soon finished those two off.

Meanwhile, after a brief fistfight, Joe's large, calloused fist found the last upright attacker's ugly face, instantly knocking him out cold.

'You took your bloody time, didn't ya?' said Shane, spitting blood as he spoke.

'I thought you could handle it,' retorted Joe. Both men hugged one another and chuckled.

Then, shoving Young Chris and Curly aside, Morgan pulled all six-foot-six of himself up and produced a whopping great big Bowie knife.

'WATCH OUT!' warned little Bob at the top of his lungs, who'd remained anxiously under the table watching.

'Robert! Get here at once!' demanded his mum, now realising where he was. Scrambling from his hideaway, he went and clung to her tightly.

Joe went to confront Morgan.

'Leave him to me!' ordered Shane, stepping in front and using his arm to move his friend back. The rest of Fletcher's boys could only watch – too injured or scared to move.

Morgan lunged at Shane, cursing him as he did, but using his martial arts skills, Shane kicked the knife right out of the coward's hand, sending it spinning through the air before landing with a resounding clang. Then, after the pair exchanged a few bruising punches, the ex-Special Forces soldier executed an *usher geri* (back-kick), sending his foe crashing against the bar before crumpling to the floor. He began to get up but, opening his eyes, saw Shane straddled over him, ready to strike again, and thought better of it.

Then, in the silence, Sam Grafton's voice rang out again: 'STOP THIS MADNESS!'

'It's over!' Shane assured him, leaning over Morgan to

fetch his Stetson from the bar top. Then, looking across to his Traveller friends, he said, 'Come on – let's go.'

'Well, who's gonna pay for all this mess!' complained the owner as the small group were about to leave.

'Get Fletcher to pay for it,' replied Joe. 'I'll be damned if I'm gonna foot the bill when his rabble fuckin' started it!'

At that, battered and bruised, Shane led the way out the door.

'I haven't had this much fun in a long time!' said Joe, putting his arm around Shane.

CHAPTER SEVENTEEN

Back at the caravan, Marian immediately nursed Shane's wounds, despite his refusal to begin with, which he appreciated. No broken bones, thankfully, but plenty of bruises and a few cuts to his face. Her huge knockers bobbing up and down in front of him helped take his mind off the stinging pain when she applied the TCP, though. Her husband came away from Grafton's with far fewer injuries. Marian told him to take a couple of Paracetamol, which he happily washed down with a large whisky.

Despite their injuries, the pair were in a buoyant mood, but at the same time, under no illusion that this would be the end of it. As the phrase goes, they may have won the battle, but they had yet to win the war! Or something like that.

Fletcher arrived first class at Gatwick late in the evening that day. He'd had a lovely break with his wife in the south of Spain and was full of the joys of Spring – well, summer. He had expected that the thorn in his side, Shane, would have been taken care of by now, so he could crack on with business as usual and turf those squatters – as he referred to them – out and start selling his luxury properties.

To say the boss was disappointed upon hearing the next morning that not only was Shane still around but had also humiliated his 'boys' is a gross understatement. He was fuming! And to make matters worse, he'd received a phone call earlier from his Superintendent chum to say that he'd checked the criminal database and a cowboy by the name of Shaun wasn't on it!

'I give you morons one simple task to complete, and you can't even do that!' barked Fletcher from behind his Portakabin office desk as his injured and dejected 'boys' trembled to the sound of their boss's stern voice. There was a pause. 'I can't believe how one man could defeat all six of you –'

'Two – two men, Boss!' interjected Curly, correcting him. 'Joe Starrett stepped in to –'

'Did I ask you to speak?' snapped the boss.

Curly just shook his head fearfully.

'No! So shut the fuck up!'

'In fairness, Boss,' said his foreman, Morgan, 'he used Kung-fu, or whatever it was, on us –'

'I don't give a flying fuck if it was Steven-fuckin'-

Seagull (he did pronounce his name wrong)! You didn't do what I asked!' Another pause. 'I've not had one fuckin' sale! Not one!' squawked Fletcher, referring to his newly built luxury homes. 'And I probably won't either, all the while those stinking – fuckin' – Gypsies and that fuckin' cowboy remain here!' The others just listened, not daring to open their mouths and speak again. 'Get the fuck outta here – all of you – while I figure out what to do next!' His boys got up and began to leave. 'Morgan! You stay here.'

Fletcher waited for the last one to exit and close the door – he trusted those pissheads about as far as he could throw them. Then, speaking confidentially in a troubled voice, he said: 'I've borrowed a shit-load of money to build these luxury properties, and if I don't start fuckin' selling them soon and making a profit, the people I owe money to aren't gonna be best pleased, if you get my drift!' Mirroring his boss's grave look, Morgan slowly nodded, knowing exactly what he meant. 'The Italians would simply shoot you in the back of the head when you least expected it. Game over! Dead before you know it!' There was a momentary deathly silence. 'But the Turks.' He shook his head with a look of dread. 'They wanna torture the hell outta ya first!' He looked directly into Morgan's eyes. 'I can't take pain, Morgan. Do you hear?' His right-hand man nodded quickly this time. 'I can't! I just can't!' Morgan just listened, wondering what he'd say next – he had a good idea, though. 'I have no choice but to hire a hitman!'

After a tense moment, Morgan dared to ask: 'Do you know such a person?'

Fletcher didn't hesitate to answer. 'Yes – I do. Stark Wilson!' He said it in a way that suggested he'd used his services before, and a glazed look befell him as if remembering something ghastly from the past: twelve months prior, in the south of Spain, Fletcher had met up with the newly retired British farmer whose land he wished to buy. At first, the stubborn farmer refused to sell the rest of his land to the pushy developer. But as soon as one of Fletcher's cronies pointed a firearm at his head, he didn't hesitate. And, under duress, he signed his land away for a measly sum. It was supposed to end there, but the trigger-happy gunman's weapon accidentally – or so he says – went off, blowing the farmer's brains out. The unstable shooter's name was, you've guessed it, Stark Wilson. The farmer's body is now buried somewhere in the Tabernas Desert (also known as 'Badlands' because of its barren and rugged landscape closely resembling the American West).

'Mr Fletcher ... Mr Fletcher!' repeated his foreman, who he could tell was in a stupor.

'What?' suddenly replied his boss grumpily as his focus returned sharply to the present with a start. 'I'll call him now,' he said with urgency. 'Not a word to

anyone – do you hear?!'

Morgan nodded sharply, 'Of course!'

Fletcher punched a nameless number on his mobile contacts list. Then waited.

Even the boss seemed a little on edge as he raised his slightly shaky finger above the big red button as if he might change his mind and end the call abruptly. But a moment later, a man's unforgettable husky Glaswegian voice answered.

Fletcher took a sharp intake of breath and, speaking in a business-like tone, said: 'I have a job for you in the UK. Get the next available flight to Gatwick. There will be someone waiting for you upon your arrival.' The call then ended.

Wiping the sweat from his brow, Fletcher addressed his somewhat anxious right-hand man: 'Get yourself off to Gatwick and wait in the arrivals lounge for the next flight from Glasgow –'

'But …' began Morgan, before thinking twice about making excuses. 'Sure, Boss!' There was a pause. 'But I don't even know what he looks like.'

'Make a big fuckin' sign with the fella's name on it, ya dipstick, and he'll find you.'

Morgan nodded with a slight grimace. Whether that was from the pain he was still in from the beating he took the day before or that he just couldn't be arsed to go, who knows? Probably both.

'Besides, you can't miss him: he's got a great big fuckin' ugly scar right across his right cheek!'

Morgan nodded reluctantly again and got up to leave. 'I'll go and fetch him now.'

'I would've asked one of the others,' remarked Fletcher, 'but I can't rely on 'em.' Then, when Morgan was almost out the door. 'Oh, and Morgan!' Morgan stopped to listen. 'Be careful what you say to him ... he's got a short fuse.'

'Right, choo are!' answered Morgan, now looking forward to it even less. He then closed the door behind him and headed for his vehicle.

Fletcher interlocked his fingers and placed his hands upon his head, muttering: 'Shit! What have I done?! Heaven help us!'

CHAPTER EIGHTEEN

Later that day, around seven, a silver Mercedes-Benz coupé pulled up outside Grafton's. It was hard to see who was inside because of the tinted windows, but shortly afterwards, Morgan stepped out of the driver's side, appearing slightly uneasy, while a similar-aged man stepped out from the passenger side. He was of average build and height, well-tanned, with dark, lank hair, which his shades kept in place atop his head, and wore a tatty grey suit without a tie. He also wore a menacing-looking scar on his face, which was so big that even those inside the cafe could easily see it.

Morgan opened the boot and removed the man's small, battered suitcase for him.

'Fletcher will meet with you in the morning,' advised Morgan. 'Enjoy your stay.' There were no smiles from either man. And once Morgan handed the passenger his luggage, he promptly got back in the car and drove off.

While Morgan drove to Gatwick to pick up Stark Wilson, Fletcher booked him a room at Grafton's.

As Stark Wilson (not likely his real name) was entering the café, wheeling his suitcase, the 'Ugly Sisters' were on their way out.

'We're closed!' the barman, Will Atkey, called out from within the café as he began lifting chairs onto tables, ready to clean the floor.

The owner had left earlier to care for his daughter, and since the bar remained closed due to the repair work needed after the damage caused the day before, Atkey now helped out elsewhere.

Atkey opened his mouth to repeat what he had said, then hastily stopped himself when he noticed the stranger was carrying a suitcase.

'Sorry,' apologised Atkey, straightening up. 'I was expecting you earlier, and I thought perhaps you'd missed your flight and weren't coming today after all.'

Stark just stood there for a moment, poker-faced, as if weighing him up. What had Fletcher told him about the new guest? 'Traffic!' he eventually said in his thick Glaswegian accent.

'Yeah, it can be a nightmare on the M25,' replied Atkey, trying his darndest not to stare at the Scottish man's scar.

The guest continued to stare.

'... Well – I – erm – expect you wanna get settled into your room,' nervously continued Atkey after an awkward moment. 'Mr Grafton, the owner, isn't here, but I can show you to your room.'

'Any coffee on the go?' asked Stark as he righted a chair that Atkey had only moments before placed upon the table.

'Well – erm ...' hesitantly began Atkey, just about picking out the word 'coffee' among the stranger's garbled sentence.

'And I could do with a hot meal,' added Stark almost expectantly as he sat down and made himself comfortable.

Plucking up the courage, Atkey answered, 'Unfortunately, the chef has just left ...' Then, as if remembering what his boss, Grafton, had said about making sure the new guest was well looked after, he continued with, 'But I'm sure I can rustle up something for you, sir.'

'Good man.'

Atkey quickly went and fetched the stranger a coffee. The cup shook slightly as he handed it to him.

'So, how was Glasgow?'

'Wet.'

Atkey feigned a half-smile (he was never one for smiling much anyway). 'So, what brings you here then?' he asked, attempting to make polite conversation.

'Business,' answered Stark with a slight scowl. 'My business!' He then casually removed a cigarette from its pack and placed it between his lips.

Atkey was about to ask him not to smoke but instead said, 'I'll go and turn the microwave on!' and, turning sharply on his heels, hurried away.

The following day, around 10 am, Fletcher and his boys rolled up outside Grafton's, and all five piled into the bar, where Stark Wilson was already there waiting for them, drinking coffee. Upon Fletcher's insistence, the premises, including the café, remained closed to the public.

Grafton greeted Fletcher with no more than a nod as he entered, pissed off that he was losing a morning's takings but was too frightened to make a fuss. He, too, lived in fear of Fletcher and his unsavoury connections and what they might do if he got on the wrong side of him.

Grafton and his few remaining staff members stayed out of the way while Fletcher ran his covert meeting, and he and his boys helped themselves to drinks behind the bar. But there was no frivolity on this occasion: this was strictly business – the 'removals business'! And so, after brief introductions, Fletcher immediately began plotting the squatter's demise.

Meeting over, as Red Marlin, Curly, and Young Chris made their way out the door, Stark leaned towards Fletcher and quietly said: 'Did you remember to bring the piece?'

Fletcher nodded and, gesturing to Morgan, just said,

'Give it to him.' Opening his tatty black briefcase, which looked older than he was, he slipped Stark the loaded weapon under the table, which he promptly slid down the back of his trousers and covered with his jacket.

As Fletcher's boys were getting into the back of the Range Rover, the conversation turned to Stark:

'So, what d'ya make of that Stark fella then?' asked Curly.

'He's not playing with a full deck if ya ask me?' said Young Chris.

'I reckon I could 'ave him!' boasted Curly.

The others laughed.

'Oh, yeah, like you did with the cowboy the other day!' said Red, scoffing.

'Well, I would've if I hadn't slipped on some beer!' promptly came Curly's feeble excuse.

'More like your piss!' joked Red to more laughter.

Just then, Fletcher and Morgan came outside looking sombre, which immediately silenced the others.

CHAPTER NINETEEN

A few days passed by, and word soon spread about the newcomer in town and, along with it, speculation as to why he was there in the first place – especially when seen hanging about with Fletcher and his 'boys'. By the way that he dressed and carried himself, he didn't look like the typical construction worker. Fletcher's lawyer, a business partner, or a relative, perhaps, some suggested.

Shane had a far more sinister suspicion as to why the stranger was in town, but he didn't want to alarm his hosts any more than they already felt. He had a nose for such things. Call it a gut instinct. But whatever the reason was, it wasn't a good one.

Shane's suspicion first arose when he saw the suited stranger strolling along the beach puffing on a cigarette early one evening, stopping every so often to observe each of the caravans in turn. He seemed far more interested in those and the comings and goings of the Travellers than he did in the beautiful shoreline and yachts out at sea, which struck him as odd. Shane was riding one of Marian's horses along the water's edge when he first spotted him. After observing him for a while, he thought about approaching him to find out who he was – and get a better sense of what he might be up to, but the overdressed man started heading away.

There was an ill wind approaching, far more malevolent than before, and Shane knew it! And his nasty suspicion became a reality a lot sooner than he'd thought: that very evening, around 11.30 pm, Henry Shipstead's large static caravan caught on fire while everyone inside was sound asleep in their beds. Luckily for him and his family, his neighbour, who had remained awake watching television, saw the blaze and immediately sounded the alarm. Other Travellers soon came to their rescue also, banging on the doors and windows as loudly as they could to alert those inside. Thankfully, amid the acrid smoke, all the occupants, including children and a pet dog, managed to escape.

The Travellers tried desperately to douse the flames with hose pipes and buckets of water. But it was all to no avail, and in seemingly no time at all, the Shipsteads' once cherished home was completely engulfed in flames and destroyed.

Hopeless phone calls to the emergency services took place, but by the time the fire brigade arrived and extinguished the flames, all that was left was a smouldering shell. Henry Shipstead and his family were lucky to be alive: minutes later, they would've been dead!

Despite the Travellers' fervent protests, no one on the police investigation team believed their claims that Luke Fletcher was culpable – or they chose not to listen. The brief investigation hastily concluded that the cause of the fire was an unextinguished cigarette and reported it as 'Accidental Fire Damage'.

Understandably distraught and angry at the police findings, especially as Mr Shipman and his wife swore blind they didn't smoke a cigarette that evening, with nowhere of their own to live, despite being offered accommodation in the other Travellers' already cramped caravans, the Shipsteads decided to abandon their charred plot and relocate somewhere else.

The other Travellers waved them goodbye as they set off in their two undamaged vehicles minus the caravan. Tears ran down the cheeks of many of the womenfolk – and some of the menfolk too before they quickly wiped them away to maintain their macho look.

Marian was one of those who struggled with her composure as she waved goodbye to the children staring through the rear windows and watched their sad little faces as they waved back.

'Which one of us is gonna be next?!' voiced Frank

Torrey with grave concern.

No response came, but they were all thinking the same thing.

'Well, I'm not sure my family and I can take much more of this!' continued Torrey after a beat. Then, directing his words of disquiet at Joe Starrett, 'It's all very well you telling us to remain strong. But look where that got poor Henry and his family.' He shook his head. 'If it carries on this way, we'll be joining them! You can be sure of that!'

'Look – we don't know for sure that the fire was Fletcher's doing,' said Joe, more calmly. 'It could've been an accident. Both of 'em smoked like chimneys!'

'Oh, come on, Joe!' sharply responded Lew Johnson, frowning. 'You know damn well as much as we do that it was Fletcher.'

'Probably ...' concurred Joe with a slight up and down of the head.

Sat outside Grafton's bar, Fletcher and his boys watched with glee and gloated at the Shipstead family's departure, waving at them mockingly. Curly even dropped his trousers and mooned them as they drove past at speed.

'If that fire doesn't send the others packing, I don't know what will,' commented Red Marlin, grinning.

'Well, it's best not to jump to conclusions too quickly,' advised Fletcher, ever cautious. 'Some of those families, like the Starretts' – he curled his lip – 'are stubborn bastards and don't get scared quite as easily! And they'll be much more vigilant now.'

The others listened to their boss in agreement.

'We need to keep the pressure up. Remove Joe Starrett and the rest'll scatter like a house of cards!' continued Fletcher smugly.

'Two families down, four more to go, eh, boss?' said Young Chris to no response, just a glare from Fletcher.

'Has anyone got a light?' asked Stark Wilson to much laughter.

CHAPTER TWENTY

'They were a good family,' said Marian, as she, Joe, Bob, and Shane walked solemnly home.

'Yeah,' agreed Joe. 'They certainly didn't deserve that.'

'None of you do,' interjected Shane, who had his arm around the lad, comforting him.

'We now need to keep on our guard more so than ever!' exclaimed Joe, quickening his pace. 'And we'll keep all the windows shut at night – even if the weather is hot and sticky.'

Marian didn't question it, just kept on walking briskly to keep up with him. The thought that their caravan could be next, never far from their minds.

'Can we play gunslingers when we get home, Shane?' asked the boy, quick to forget about any troubles.

'Sure, we can, Bob,' he replied with a growing smile.

For the next few nights, after the remaining Travellers had retired and gone to sleep, much to their displeasure, they were rudely awakened by two pickup trucks, driving at high speed, revving their engines loudly and playing rock music at full capacity. Up and down the dirt track, they raced for quite a while, intentionally disturbing the peace. Children cried, and dogs barked and whimpered out of fear! It was another of Fletcher's dirty tactics to get rid of them.

Not daring to leave the relative safety of their caravans after dark, one morning the Travellers awoke to find their front gardens decimated: picket fences snapped or flattened, flowers crushed and destroyed, and lawns wrecked by numerous tyre marks!

Fletcher's boys even had the gall to secretly plant a kilo of hash inside old Lew Johnson's shed, in an attempt to frame him for possession of a class B drug (Fletcher was too stingy to part with any cocaine). But by the time the cops arrived, the Travellers had already smoked it. It disappeared in a puff of smoke!

Fletcher was doing his darndest to rile and provoke the Travellers and cause a reaction, so Stark had an excuse to step in and 'deal with them', claiming self-defence if need be. And, in the week that followed, it would cost one of the Travellers their life!

Enough was enough, and despite having no clear video evidence to prove who the culprits were, early one morning, Joe Starrett and a few of the other angry male Travellers confronted Fletcher about the offences outside his showroom office. He denied the whole thing, of course, and in no uncertain terms told them to piss off, threatening to call the police if they didn't do so immediately. A bitter argument ensued, but facing the threat of eviction, with no proof of purchase or knowledge of the farmer's whereabouts, fearing for their already tenuous grip on their land, they soon gave up and left.

Shane was unaware of this. He had been jogging along the shoreline as usual and had a confrontation of his own to deal with.

Dripping with sweat and wearing only the skimpiest of shorts, cowboy boots, and his Stetson hanging from his neck, the protagonist suddenly stopped in his tracks. Up ahead, just beyond one of the beach's many groynes, he could see someone's white, skinny arse bobbing up and down faster than a jackrabbit.

Moving closer, he realised it was the young drug dealer, shagging one of the 'Ugly Sisters'. She had her eyes closed, and he had his head down, so neither was aware of the cowboy's shadow suddenly looming over them.

Shane planted his big boot upon the guy's pale arse. The girl suddenly screamed in ecstasy. Then opened her eyes and screamed in terror.

'Caught ya!' snarled Shane, removing his sandy boot and allowing the embarrassed pair to cover themselves up. *'Leave!'* he then told the girl. 'I need to have a serious word with this low-life-piece-of-shit!' Sensing the lad was about to run, he grabbed his shirt collar. 'Thinking of escaping, were ya?' he said before punching him on the nose, causing his eyes to water and his nose to bleed. 'Sit the fuck down!' The dazed young man murmured something and dropped to the sand in pain.

'Leave him be, you fuckin' bastard!' yelled the 'Ugly Sister' from a few metres away.

'I told you to "leave"! NOW GO!' Fearing for her safety, she turned and ran, stumbling on the uneven sand.

Then, turning his attention to the whimpering lad and raising his fist again, he said, 'Now, you listen to me carefully!'

'Don't hit me! Please don't hit me!' begged the lad, cowering.

'Listen! I know you're a drug dealer – and it's no use denying it,' continued Shane, purple-faced with anger.

'So what?' came the lad's curt response.

'You caused a young girl to overdose and nearly lose her life, that's what!'

'Well, she survived, didn't she?' the uncaring lad replied cockily as he gradually slid his bottom backwards.

'Why you ...' Shane was about to strike him again, but this time the slippery devil was too quick and managed to get up and create a little distance between them.

Shane moved towards him, but the lad suddenly pulled a short-bladed knife on him.

'Fuck off, whoever you are, or I'll stab you!' threatened the nervous, trembly-voiced lad, waving the knife frantically around.

'Put the knife down!' calmly said Shane as he edged forward slightly.

'Come any closer, and you're *dead,* d'ya hear me?!'

Losing his patience, Shane reached behind his back and pulled his Glock 17 from his waistband and pointed it at the stupid boy. 'I said "Drop the fuckin' knife"!' Since the fire incident, Shane had always carried his firearm with him.

The boy/lad didn't hesitate and, with his bravado all but disappeared, he immediately dropped the knife out of his trembling hand, which landed partly buried in the sand.

'Now – on your fuckin' knees!' ordered the ex-sergeant.

The shit-scared lad, whose groin area was now soaking wet from peeing himself, did as ordered and began jabbering excessively, worried for his life. 'Don't kill me!' he kept repeating.

Glancing around to make sure no one was watching, grabbing a large tuft of the lad's greasy hair, Shane shoved the barrel of the gun into his mouth and partly down his throat to stop him talking, almost knocking his two front teeth out in the process. 'You have a simple choice, young man. Either you head back to Manchester or wherever you crawled out from immediately, or I will kill you! Do you understand?!'

Gagging, the lad nodded. 'And if you take my advice, you'll pack this lark in. Or you'll either wind up dead or in prison, where instead of a pistol down your throat, you'll have someone twice your size shoving his big, fat cock down there!' To emphasise his point, Shane shoved the barrel farther down his throat.

Then, removing the gun to the sound of more uncontrollable gagging, immediately followed by coughing and spluttering, Shane said: 'Now be on your way!' He noticed the lad glancing toward his man-bag he'd left over by the groyne. 'Leave that!' he demanded. And as the humiliated criminal turned to leave, Shane helped him on his way by kicking him up the arse. 'Don't ever let me see you again!'

Soon after the lad had hurried away, Shane unzipped his grubby bag, and sure enough, among his few possessions – headphones, smelly underwear, a toothbrush and paste – were several small, clear zippered bags of class A drugs, which he wasted no time in destroying.

Shane hoped that by frightening him, the young fellow would see the error of his ways, but he doubted it.

CHAPTER TWENTY-ONE

It was the end of the season. There was a cold chill in the air, and the rain hit hard. The summer heatwave was over.

'The rain'll do the flowers good,' said Joe Starrett.

'Yeah – what remains of 'em!' replied Marian, still bitter about the damage the senseless thugs had done to her lovely garden.

Shane entered the caravan soaked to the bone. He'd just finished fixing the last of the broken fences. 'All done!' he said, removing his Stetson and giving it a shake.

A few days had passed since the tête-à-tête with the foolish young drug dealer, whom he hadn't seen since – he'd got the message loud and clear.

'Come and sit down, Shane,' said Marian. 'I've saved you some breakfast – I expect you're hungry.'

'Thanks!' he replied, grateful.

Joe threw Shane the tea towel he was holding to dry himself off, which gave him an excuse not to have to dry the rest of the dishes.

Feeling ravenous, he quickly wiped his face and patted himself down, then promptly went and sat at the dining table, eager to fill his belly.

'There ya go! Get stuck in!' said Marian, plonking his plate of slightly dried-up food in front of him. 'I'll make you a nice cuppa!'

Despite her wearing a woolly jumper, the sudden temperature change made her nipples as hard as bullets. Shane quickly averted his gaze and began tucking into his brekkie.

'I doubt that'll be the last of our troubles,' commented Joe, referring to the damaged fences and flower beds.

I doubt it either, thought Shane. He didn't say it, though, not wishing to add to their angst by agreeing.

'I found out who that stranger is!' continued Joe. 'Will Atkey told me.'

'Will Atkey?' Shane asked, trying to remember.

'The barman at Grafton's,' quickly said Joe, reminding him. Shane acknowledged with a slow nod. 'He overheard a conversation between him and a few of Grafton's boys. Stark Wilson, they call him. And a mean son-of-a-gun if ever there was! He was in the armed forces like you, once, apparently.' Shane didn't beg to differ. Retired or not, he still kept his membership in the elite SAS a secret. 'He bragged how he'd killed men with his bare hands!'

'Well, it's best to avoid him,' merely offered Shane before shovelling another mouthful of lukewarm food into his gob. He was hungry, and it was hard to concentrate with Marian's doorstoppers for nipples screaming, 'Look at us! We're *here!'*

'Now I'm even more scared,' she suddenly voiced. 'Look, why the hell don't we just pack up and leave like the Lewis family before one of us gets killed?!'

'Because then Fletcher has won!' Joe shot back with a look of consternation as if to say, banish the thought.

'It's not a game, Joe Starrett!' she countered with.

'No, I know.' He went to put his arm around her, but she stepped aside and found himself hugging only the air instead. 'Where do you suggest we go?' She didn't answer. She continued staring at the wall in front of her with her arms folded. '... Look at me, Marian.' Reluctantly, she did as he asked. 'This is our home now, and you know that I'll always protect you and Robert!'

She smiled faintly and nodded her acknowledgement, desperately wanting to believe him – needing to believe him. Then, changing the topic of conversation completely, as if it had never happened, she said, 'It's time our lazy boy woke up. And, moving briskly towards his bedroom, she yelled, 'ROBERT! IT'S TIME YOU GOT OUT OF BED!'

Later that morning, tensions rose again when Fletcher's

Range Rover pulled up outside the Starretts' property.

Cautiously pulling the net curtain aside to peek, Marian let out a short gasp, saying, *'Fuck!'* Continuing to stare out of the rain-streaked window, she added, 'They're here!'

'Whose here?' asked Joe, promptly getting up from his seat and moving towards the window. The boy abandoned his bowl of cereal and also went to look. Shane remained at the dining table, calmly finishing his cup of tea.

'What the hell do they want now?' said Marian, full of angst.

No one answered, but after a brief moment of hesitation, Joe moved swiftly to the front door, yanking it open, ready to face his arch-enemy. Bob followed him until Marian quickly told him to sit back down again.

Dressed in ominous-looking dark suits and shades, despite the lack of sunshine, Morgan got out of the vehicle first, followed by the rest of Fletcher's boys, including Stark. Fletcher's right-hand man hastily opened a blue and white striped golfing umbrella, then opened the front passenger door for the boss to step out.

Continuing to shield Fletcher from the rain, the two stepped forward towards the gate, while the others remained in line, getting wet. The relentless rain didn't stop Stark, though, from removing a cigarette and lighting it. He then took great delight in blowing big puffs of smoke into the air, as if goading the occupants into believing that their caravan could be next to catch fire. The big smirk on his face definitely suggested it.

'Stop right there!' demanded Joe in a raised voice, rarely heard. 'We don't want any trouble!'

'Go and play in your room, Robert!' ordered his mum, sensing danger.

'Oh, but Mu-um!' he whined, dropping his spoon into the bowl with a splash.

'Go!' she repeated, which he did, stomping his feet every step of the way.

'I have merely come to serve you an eviction order, which I thought I'd do in person,' smugly said Fletcher.

'Eviction order?! On whose authority?' Joe suddenly looked stone-cold worried.

'The KCC, of course.'

Joe opened his mouth to speak, but nothing came out. He held onto the railings for support. Such was the shock.

Fletcher was loving this. 'You seem surprised, Mr Starrett – shocked even,' he continued to say with glee.

'You're lying!' Joe finally spurted out.

'I assure you I am not. Look – I have it here!' Reaching into his inner pocket, he triumphantly brought the envelope forth and waved it about. 'Would you like me to hand it to you, or shall I just pop it in your mail box?'

He gestured as if to post it into the rusty mailbox by the gate.

Joe remained silent, desperately trying to curb the pent-up anger inside him.

'I'll pop it in here – save you getting wet!' Fletcher answered for him, suiting his actions to his words. *'There!'*

Then, after a moment, 'I own this fuckin' land!' angrily stated Joe.

'Well, Mr Starrett, that is something you will have to prove in a court of law!'

Just then, Shane stepped into view from behind the caravan to offer his support. All eyes suddenly fixed upon him.

'I can handle this myself, Shane!' Joe immediately told him. He remained there all the same.

'No need to concern yourselves – there's nothing more that needs to be said for now,' interjected Fletcher with a fixed smile. 'I'm leaving now anyway. I promised my wife and children I'd take them out for lunch – and she gets quite upset if I'm late.'

All the while, Shane and Stark eyeballed each other, each measuring the other up, each waiting for the other to make the first move.

Fletcher started to turn away, then sharply turned back and, pulling an ugly face, barked, 'You've got one week to get your stinkin' fuckin' ugly selves and your flea-ridden fuckin' animals along with your crappy fuckin' caravans off this land!'

Just then, Marian came charging past her husband, brandishing a sawn-off shotgun, screaming, 'I've heard just about enough from your fuckin' gape, Fletcher!' Then, after momentarily steadying herself on the top step, she pointed the weapon at him.

'WHOA! WHOA! WHOA!' everybody, including Joe and Shane, yelled in panic as most scrambled for cover. Still standing next to her, Joe immediately used his right forearm to knock the barrel of the gun skyward. A bright flash and a loud bang followed as the explosive went off!

'For *Christ's sake,* woman, what on *God's* earth d'ya think you are doin'?!' he said as he snatched the gun from her in a panic.

While Fletcher and his boys hastily got back into the Rover, Marian hollered: ''Go on, that's it, piss-off, the lot of yis!' Then, after a deep breath, promptly added, 'And we all know that you are the one responsible for setting the caravan alight, Fletcher!' And before the fearful passengers could even close all the doors, the vehicle sped off, leaving dust and Fletcher's abandoned umbrella in its wake!

'Are you *fuckin'* crazy, Marian?!' Joe yelled after her as she stormed back inside the caravan, and he followed. 'You've just played *right* into Fletcher's hands!'

'I wished I'd have bloody-well killed the bastard!' she replied, full of rage still.

The moment Shane heard them arguing, he thought better of interfering and made his way back around the caravan again to his quarters. Little Bob put his headphones on – an action he did a lot in this household!

'They could have you arrested for attempted murder!'

'Good! Fuckin'-well let 'em! I don't care anymore!'

'Don't say that! You know you don't mean that, Marian!' There was a brief pause. 'What good will it do, if you're in prison, *eh?* Think about our son!'

Marian burst into tears. 'I'm sorry! I don't know what came over me! Oh, what are we gonna do, Joe?!' she lamented.

'Nothing!' came Joe's swift response. 'God damn, nothing!'

CHAPTER TWENTY-TWO

A couple of days later, during the twilight hours, Frank Torrey and Earnie Wright were talking by the roadside a short distance from Grafton's.

'... Are you coming for a tipple or not, Frank?'

Frank seemed reluctant and shook his head. 'No - I'll give it a miss – Fletcher and his boys are probably there!'

'So what? You ain't scared of them, are ya?'

'No – but –'

'I ain't scared of them!' continued Earnie, getting hot under the collar. He spat on the ground, accidentally smearing Frank's boot with slimy gob, which neither of them noticed. 'If I wanna goddamn drink, I'm certainly not gonna let those bunch of losers stop me!'

Saying that, with his chest puffed out, Earnie, who had already had a fair bit to drink before coming out, turned and began to walk away, staggering slightly as he did.

'D'ya think that's wise, Earnie, when you know they're gunning for us?!' warned his friend, remaining put.

Turning his head as he continued to walk in the

direction of Grafton's, Earnie plainly replied, 'Nope – probably not!'

'You're a fool!'

Shortly afterwards, the little rascal, Ollie Johnson, came shooting past Frank Torrey towards home with a mobile phone gripped tightly in his hand.

'Hold up! Why are you running so fast?!' Frank questioned the boy, but he didn't stop to answer.

Five or so minutes earlier, Fletcher was in the back of his Range Rover, parked on the verge of the road not far beyond Grafton's, receiving a blowjob when suddenly a flash went off outside the window. Dazed, Young Chris looked up, eyes open wide, with the boss's cock still in his mouth. While Fletcher, shocked and horrified that one of the Travellers' kids had taken a snap of them in the act, yanked Chris off him by the hair, lowered the window, and, angry as hell, leaned out shouting, *'Oi!* Come back here, you little *shit!'* Then, promptly getting out of the car, while hastily zipping his trousers back up, he began chasing after him, shouting, 'If you dare show that photo to anyone ...!' But by then, the mischievous lad was already well ahead of him.

Now the Travellers had a bargaining chip. But that, at most, embarrassing photo, would prove inconsequential, as things were about to take a turn for the worse – a lot worse!

Panting and cussing under his breath, the middle-aged

boss almost immediately stopped running and continued walking towards Grafton's. Ashamed and embarrassed, Young Chris quickly followed his abusive boss.

Soon after Fletcher and Young Chris entered the bar, Earnie Wright sauntered inside. He'd only taken one step beyond the door when Red and Morgan, almost in unison, growled, 'What the fuck d'you think you are doin' here?!' Or words to that effect.

'I've come to get a drink,' answered Ernie, daring to take another step. 'It's a free country, ain't it? And I'll do as I goddamn please!'

Business had been quiet of late, and the owner had left Will Atkey in charge again. While pouring Fletcher a generous measure of whisky, the meek bartender went to open his mouth to speak, but Morgan spoke for him: 'The bar's closed!'

'It sure doesn't look that way to me,' argued Earnie, gazing around the room at Fletcher and his boys getting drunk.

Stark, who until now had remained quiet, stepped away from the bar to confront Wright square on. 'You heard the man,' he said with a snarl. 'We don't want your sort in here! Now fuck off, Pikey!'

'You fuck off!' bravely began Wright.

'Take one more step and it'll be your last!' warned the hitman, pulling his jacket aside to reveal the handle of a

SIG-Sauer P226 protruding from the front of his trousers.

'I ain't scared of you!' boldly replied the Traveller, remaining defiant in front of the open doorway.

A fleeting glance over his left shoulder towards Fletcher told Stark all he needed to know, and, as Earnie unwisely took another step towards the bar, the hired killer withdrew his weapon with the swiftness of a gunfighter in a Spaghetti Western and blasted him through the chest, sending him hurtling back out the door and ending up spreadeagled on his back, dead!

Some of the bar's occupants looked aghast, while others appeared to smirk.

Fletcher even seemed happy. Quickly downing his whisky, he said, 'You two!' indicating towards Curly and Young Chris. 'Get the body back in here now!'

The bartender continued drying glasses as if nothing had happened – he even hummed a song to himself.

'He got what he deserved!' voiced Morgan.

Upon hearing the gun blast, Atkey's wife, Melisa, and Mr Weir, the chef, who had been sitting idly about chatting and drinking coffee alone in the café, came rushing into the bar to find out what had happened. But Red quickly ushered the inquisitive pair away.

All the while, Stark remained where he stood for the moment, calm as can be, with the smoking gun still in his hand.

Curly nearly vomited as they took one of Earnie Wright's limp legs each and dragged him back inside, leaving a trail of blood behind.

'Did you see anybody outside?!' asked Fletcher, panicking slightly.

'Erm – yes,' said Curly, straight-faced. There was an anxious pause. 'The deceased!'

'You idiot!' said Morgan, tutting and shaking his head.

'I don't think so,' answered Young Chris unconvincingly.

'What d'ya mean, you don't think so? Did you see anyone or not?' asked Morgan, hastily moving towards the door to check for himself.

'Well, I was busy picking up the ...' tried to explain Young Chris.

'Same here,' confessed Curly.

The pair let go of the corpse's legs, causing one dull thud after another.

Morgan soon returned, looking concerned. 'I just saw one of the Gypo's running like the clappers towards the Traveller site. He may have witnessed what happened!'

Frank Torrey did indeed witness what happened: after the boy raced past him, sensing something awry, he decided to turn around and follow Earnie to the bar. But as he approached the entrance, he happened to glance through the window and, to his horror, witnessed Stark killing his unarmed friend! And, after a sharp intake of breath, petrified, he quickly went and hid behind the side wall, desperately hoping no one had seen him, waiting for his chance to flee.

At the Starrett's Caravan:

'Was that a gunshot?!' enquired Marian, sounding alarmed as she sat bolt upright on the couch, while dogs barked outside.

'It sounded like it,' replied Joe, sitting next to her, checking the racing results. 'It's probably from the Lydd Firing Ranges!'

'What – at this time of the day?!' She turned towards him with a frown as if to say, 'Don't be stupid!'

'Well, possibly,' he said with a slight shrug. 'I expect that the military has target practice when it's dark as well!'

'But there was only one shot,' she continued to argue. 'There's usually lots of shooting!'

'You have a point,' he agreed, getting up to look out the front window.

'Where's Shane, by the way?' she suddenly asked, realising that she hadn't seen him for a while.

'I dunno – he just said he was gonna see an old friend about something or other,' he answered vaguely but truthfully before returning to sit down again.

'Oh,' she uttered. 'I wonder who that is then ...'

Then, as if noticing for the first time that their son

wasn't about either, he asked: 'Where's Bob?'

'I sent him to bed early for being rude to me,' she replied, still wondering where Shane had gone.

At Grafton's:

Melisa and Mr Weir were shagging inside the storeroom as usual. Atkey was out the back getting some fresh air while smoking a cigarette. Stark had also lit a fag and was now sitting at the bar, gun hidden away, pouring himself a free whiskey. Red was taking a shit. And Fletcher was still flapping about dishing out orders.

'... You know what to do with the body,' Fletcher said to Morgan. 'There'll be a meat cleaver in the kitchen!' His right-hand man grunted his affirmation and, leaving his drink at the table, set to it. 'Curly! Chris! You help him!' Now Curly vomited. 'I need to fetch some more weapons from the boot of my car – something tells me there's gonna be fireworks tonight!'

'You mean the Gypsies might come seeking revenge?!' said Curly with a hint of trepidation, wiping the puke away from his chin with the sleeve of his shirt.

'I damn-well hope so!' answered the boss as he was about to exit. 'Then we can get rid of the scum once and for all!'

CHAPTER TWENTY-THREE

When Frank Torrey finally arrived home about 8 pm, exhausted and crestfallen, his desperate laments immediately garnered the attention of everyone in the Traveller community. People came running out of their caravans to find out what the matter was. And soon a large crowd had gathered around him to listen to what he had to say.

'... Earnie Wright's dead!' cried Torrey, full of emotion.

Shocked gasps immediately followed.

'Dead?! Did he say Dead?' questioned more than one of them.

'Earnie's dead – how?' asked another, deeply concerned like the rest of them.

Wright continued to rant. 'I warned Frank not to go there ...'

'... Slow down, Frank!' said Henry Shipstead, finding it difficult, as were most, to comprehend what he was saying in his haste to tell all.

'Where!' asked Lew Johson abruptly.

'Grafton's Bar,' Torrey finally answered.

'Take a moment,' suggested Joe Starrett, but Frank kept ranting at a frenetic pace.

'... That Stark fella killed him! Shot him in cold blood! I saw it with my own eyes! The murdering bastard! And Fletcher and his boys did nothing – just stood around and let it happen, they did!'

'That was the gunshot we heard!' Marian said to Joe, who remained listening intently to Torrey.

'I wanted to intervene,' Torrey continued tearfully, 'but it was too late – the gun went off before –'

'Don't beat yourself up about it, Frank,' said Marian. 'There was nothing you could do!' She placed a hand tenderly upon his shoulder. 'Somebody get him a drink – and make it a strong one!'

'I knew it wouldn't be long before one of us got killed!' bitterly expressed Torrey, regaining some of his composure. 'Well, my family and I are not staying here any longer!' He looked towards his wife and ten kids, who were clinging to each other, frightened.

'I'll start packing!' his worried-looking wife immediately replied, quickly ushering the children back inside their caravan. Forlorn, their dad followed them.

'But Frank!' began Joe. 'If you leave, Earnie's death will be in vain!' Frank didn't answer. 'Be brave like him!'

Frank stopped at the top of the caravan steps and abruptly turned around, looking angry. 'What and get shot like him also?!'

'Let it be,' advised Joe's wife.

'We should call the police!' strongly suggested Shipstead.

It started to pour down with rain again.

'We'll do no such thing!' insisted the leader, Joe Starrett. 'I'll deal with it my way!' He turned sharply on his heels and headed for his caravan in a hurry.

'Joe!' exclaimed Marian, alarmed. 'What are you gonna do?!' He ignored her. 'Joe – come back here! Don't be a hotheaded fool!' She chased after him, while others quickly sought shelter from the rain.

'There's a time for doing nothing, and there's a time to act! Well, now's that time!' She tried to grab his arm, but he shrugged her away. 'Get off me, woman!'

'Joe, if you go to Grafton's, you'll get yourself killed! Don't you see?! That's precisely what Fletcher wants!' She continued following him into the caravan, both of them dripping wet.

'It's time Fletcher got what was coming to him!' said Joe, seething with anger. 'Where's the shotgun?' He'd searched the usual hideaway, but it wasn't there.

Marian didn't answer.

'I said, *Where's* the shotgun?!' he demanded.

'Where you last left it,' she reluctantly replied. 'You took the gun from me – remember?'

Hellbent on revenge, he dashed out the back door,

suddenly remembering he'd hidden it in the stables among the hay.

'For the love of Mary, Joe! Don't be stupid!' she yelled, distraught beyond measure.

Just then, little Bob came running out of his bedroom, concerned. 'Mum! Mum! What is it?!' he asked, sensing trouble.

'Go back to bed!' she told him immediately. 'Everything's all right.' He could see how stressed out she was, so he didn't dare argue. But not before visiting the bathroom for a tinkle.

Looking out the back door as the rain lashed down, lit by the security light, she watched her erratic man as he frantically searched among the hay, causing the horses to become agitated and frightened.

To her utter relief, Shane came in through the front door. 'Boy! That rain is heavy –'

'Shane!' she expressed, turning around abruptly to face him.

He could immediately see she was distressed. 'What is it, Marian?'

'Oh, Shane!' She ran over to him and wrapped her arms around him tightly, resting her head momentarily on his shoulder. 'Something terrible has happened!' She pulled herself slightly away from him and continued, 'Stark shot and killed poor Earnie Wright at Grafton's bar. Now Joe wants revenge!'

'Where's Joe?!' hurriedly asked Shane.

'He's out the back searching for his shotgun!' she swiftly replied.

Shane immediately ran towards the open rear door and, bypassing the steps, jumped directly onto the wet and muddy ground below. Then, without stopping, moved with haste towards the stables, one squelching boot after another, calling out, 'JOE!' Joe suddenly appeared at the entrance, brandishing the loaded shotgun. Uncharacteristically, he had the look of a madman.

'Joe! Don't do this!' strongly advised Shane, with arms outstretched.

'Get out of my way!' demanded big Joe as he barged past Shane.

'Stop him, Shane! He's gonna get himself killed!' desperately cried Marian from the top of the steps as the rain continued to pelt down.

Shane immediately grabbed Joe's bulky left arm and pulled him back. 'Do as your wife says, Joe. You're no match for Stark!'

'Well, we'll see about that!' Joe used the butt of his gun and whacked Shane against the side of his head.

'JOE!' Marian screamed. 'Have you lost your senses?!'

Again, Joe steamrolled past Shane, as he crouched slightly in pain and rubbed his sore head. But Shane wasn't about to give in. 'JOE!' he yelled. 'I don't wanna hurt cha! STOP!' But, stubborn as ever, Joe persisted in ignoring him.

He got about three long strides away when Shane rushed him from behind and, grabbing both his ankles, brought him to the ground with a big splash. Joe's shotgun immediately launched out of his hands and landed out of reach in the mud. Rising to his feet first, Shane warned Joe to stay down. Cursing, Joe pulled himself almost halfway up when Shane planted his boot on the centre of his back and shoved him onto the mucky ground again. 'I said, "stay down"!' he warned him again, but Joe was having nothing of it and, quickly rolling onto his back, he scrambled to his feet before Shane could reach him and immediately started throwing punches his way.

A moment later, Joe caught Shane with a powerful blow to his right cheek that would've knocked most other men out cold. He staggered backwards, feeling dazed, but somehow managed to remain on his feet.

'STOP IT!' begged Marian in vain as the stubborn pair exchanged more bruising blows, neither man prepared to stand down.

Bob then suddenly appeared, squeezing his head between his mum's hip and the door frame. 'STOP FIGHTING!' he yelled at the top of his voice. But even he couldn't make them see sense, and it wasn't long before blood appeared on both the weary men's faces.

The senseless fighting continued for a short while longer, until Shane finally stopped it by grabbing a nearby shovel and knocking Joe out as he tried to leave again. He had to prevent his determined friend from going to Grafton's somehow: he knew that if Joe had gone there that evening, he would've ended up dead like Earnie Wright, and he couldn't let that happen. He, and he alone, had to end this war between Fletcher and the Travellers – and end it the only way he knew how!

'I *hate* you, Shane!' yelled the boy, angry and in tears.

'Shane! Did you have to do that?!' questioned Marian, equally upset as she rushed down the steps to her unconscious husband's aid.

'He'll be okay,' Shane reassured the worried pair as rain washed the mud and blood from Joe's face. 'He should come round soon!'

Shane helped Marian carry Joe's heavy, limp body inside and lay him carefully on the sofa. He then immediately asked, 'Marian, can I borrow one of your horses?' preferring on this occasion to swap his bike for a much faster mode of transport.

This time, she didn't question anything: immediately replying, 'Yes – take Betsy! She's yours!' She knew that Shane's actions were solely to protect Joe – and also knew there was nothing she could say or do to stop him from confronting Fletcher and his boys instead.

Then, out of the blue. 'Stay away from the windows!'

Shane warned her.

She frowned but confirmed she would with a nod.

'Where are you going?' asked little Bob, to no reply.

Shane was about to exit when she called out to him, saying, 'Take good care of yourself! And give 'em *hell!'*

Shane smiled briefly and was gone.

CHAPTER TWENTY-FOUR

As Shane mounted Betsy, with his fully loaded Glock 17 nestled down the front of his soaked and muddy jeans and Joe's shotgun firmly in his grasp, he could faintly hear Joe's awakening voice, which reassured him that his friend was okay. And as the rain continued unabated, he steered the mare carefully around the caravan, mindful not to trample on any of Marian's newly planted flowers.

He had only reached the road when little Bob came running around the side of the caravan, trampling all over Marian's newly planted flowers, waving something in the air and calling out his name: 'SHANE! SHANE! DON'T FORGET THIS!'

Not wanting to upset the boy further than he had already, Shane pulled on the reins and waited for the boy to approach.

'Shane – you nearly forgot your sheriff's badge!' the wide-eyed boy told him as he handed it to his hero high up on the saddle.

Shane smiled from the heart. 'Thank you! How could I forget that!' he replied as he pinned it prominently upon his chest. 'Now you go back inside, Bobby-boy, before you catch a cold!'

'Okay,' replied little Bob as he waved Shane goodbye. 'I DON'T REALLY HATE YOU, SHANE!' he hurriedly shouted as the brave vigilante galloped away towards Grafton's.

Faster and faster the horse's powerful legs took Shane along the desolate beach road, churning up sand and grit as it did. He could ride a horse as well as any jockey in the land!

It was fast approaching 10 pm, and inside Grafton's bar, Fletcher and his boys, along with a few other tough-looking men, were starting to get restless.

'Does anyone still reckon any of those inbreds are coming?' questioned Red as he peered outside the entrance for the umpteenth time.

'Nah! They're too chicken!' answered Curly, after a moment.

'Starrett'll be here alright. You mark my words!' said the boss confidently.

'What about that Shane fella – d'ya think he'll come too?' anxiously asked Red as he returned his gaze inside the bar.

'No,' replied Fletcher assuredly again. 'Don't cha

worry about him: he'll be long gone by now ...' The others, who were mostly sitting at the bar, looked curiously at him. 'A dickie bird told me a taxi picked him up earlier today and headed in the other direction. I bet he's had enough of those filthy, stinking Gypsies, like the rest of us!' He nodded as if he was agreeing with himself. 'He's made a bit of money, and he's now decided to do the sensible thing by getting the fuck outta Dodge!'

Suddenly, several almighty explosions rang out nearby. It was so loud and powerful that the reverberations could be felt inside the bar: bottles and glasses rattled noisily behind the bar, and a few fell from tables and smashed to the floor – not to mention, windows being blown in!

'What the hell was that!' said the boss, almost falling from his perch.

'I dunno, but it sounded like it was coming from the direction of the new development!' expressed Morgan, deeply concerned as he rushed towards the entrance, followed by Curly and Young Chris.

Stark remained calmly where he was.

Red had already run outside to see. 'Oh, my god!' he shrieked as he came running back inside. 'It's on fire!'

'What's on fuckin' fire?!' demanded Fletcher.

'Your ...' He hesitated. 'Your development, Boss!' finally answered Red in a state of shock.

Morgan, Curly, and Young Chris barged past him to take a look for themselves. 'It's completely flattened!' said Young Chris loudly, upon noticing the once-imposing outline was no longer there to be seen.

'I bet it was those fuckin' Gypsies!' said Curly, hastily fumbling to remove his pistol from his waistband and almost dropping it.

Morgan sniggered, saying, 'No – that bunch of idiots wouldn't know the difference between a stick of dynamite and a stick of rock!' Then, with certainty, 'It was Shane!'

Morgan wasn't wrong about that: earlier that day, Shane had paid an old military friend a visit at the Lydd Firing Range just up the coast. And, with his help, managed to smuggle out a shit-load of self-detonating explosives!

No sooner had Morgan mentioned his name than Shane appeared from out of the haze of thick black drifting smoke, thundering towards Grafton's at breakneck speed, wearing his unmistakable Stetson, with his shotgun pointing right at them!

'Oh, Fuck!' mouthed Curly, letting out a lengthy fart.

'Quick! Get inside!' yelled Morgan as he made a mad dash for the opening. Curly immediately followed, almost throwing himself inside. Young Chris, on the other hand, thought he'd be the hero and challenge the fast-approaching lone rider. Drawing his shooter, he

took one step forward and fired it at Shane, missing by a long way off. A moment later, a much louder shot rang out. The wanna-be killer then took two steps back with a gaping bullet hole right through his abdomen from Shane's shotgun!

What a waste! thought Shane with a slight pang of regret as he watched the foolhardy lad collapse and die in front of him. But with no time for sentimentality, he pulled sharply on the reins and came to an abrupt halt. Then, before dismounting and tethering the horse to a drainpipe at the corner of the cafe, he leaned forward and, lifting one of the horse's ear bonnets, calmly reassured the horse, along with a caring pat on the neck, that everything would be all right.

'Young Chris is dead!' cried Red, daring to sneak a peek out the door once more.

Random shots instantaneously cracked and popped from within, as a few of Fletcher's boys nervously fired blindly out into the darkness – some wayward shots further smashed panes of glass, and Red had to duck low to avoid being shot.

'Hold your fire!' growled Fletcher with his hands tightly covering his ears.

Amid the smell of gunpowder smoke and other unpleasant odours, an unnerving silence quickly enveloped the edgy occupants. Then the mysterious stranger appeared in the doorway, with only one thing on his mind: payback! He held the shotgun in his left hand, the handgun in his right, and the pin of a hand grenade clenched between his teeth.

Glancing about the smoky room, Shane first noticed Will Atkey busying himself behind the bar and looking as nervous as ever. Fletcher was leaning against the end of the bar over to his right. Right next to him was Morgan. Sitting in the centre, with his back towards Shane, was the killer, Stark. Red was standing by a table on the left, where Curly sat biting his nails. There were also three other men, whom he'd never seen before, hunched over a table to the right. And, judging by the number of empty glasses scattered about the place, it appeared as if they'd all been drinking heavily, which, despite being outnumbered, was to his advantage. But on this occasion, there was no music playing, no banter, no laughter. The mood was deadly sombre.

Lowering his glance, Shane was suddenly aware of the stray black cat, pissing on him. But a violent shake of his leg soon sent it scurrying off. *Fuckin' cat!* he thought.

'Nobody shoot unless I say!' ordered Fletcher, who was one of the few unarmed.

'Is that a hand grenade in his mouth?' nervously asked Curly, shitting himself.

'Well, it ain't a fuckin' apple!' replied Red.

Shane took a confident step inside.

'Stop right there, cowboy!' advised Fletcher, shifting

his weight onto his right forearm to get a better look at him. 'You're well outnumbered, so don't try anything foolish or rash!' There was a pause. 'Where's Starrett?' Then another pause. 'Never mind! I'm sure we can sort out any disagreements or grievances we might have amicably between us.' Smiling falsely, he continued with, 'What do you care about those fuckin' Gypo's for, anyway?' Shane continued to listen, but his patience was quickly running out. 'I could do with a man of your talents working for me. And, what's more, I'll pay you triple what Starrett is paying you! What d'ya say, Shaun?'

'It's Shane, Boss!' Morgan reminded him.

'Shane, I mean,' uttered Fletcher, slightly red-faced – though that could've been the whisky.

'Ay oodent urk fur ooh ina illiyun uckin yers, ya unt!' Shane garbled as his teeth firmly gripped the grenade still.

'What did he say?' Fletcher asked Morgan.

'I think he called you a cunt, Boss!' frankly answered his right-hand man.

Fletcher snarled.

Suddenly, one of the men, who sat in a group of three, abruptly got up to leave. 'I wanna leave!'

Angered further, Fletcher snatched the pistol out of Morgan's hand and, after pointing the weapon at the departing man's head and saying, 'Let me help you!'

pulled the trigger and blew his brains out.

Brain matter and blood splattered over Curly in an instant, sending him into a frenzied panic attack as he desperately tried to brush it off his face and out of his mass of curly hair. Red had to put two firm hands on his shoulders to keep him still. 'Stop being a pussy!' he hurriedly told him as he leaned close to the perturbed lad's left ear.

Shane remained poker-faced but with his fingers firmly on the triggers. *That's one less I have to deal with!* he mused as the victim's body lay strewn across the central aisle a couple of metres in front of him. *Keep this up, and the only person I'll have to kill is Fletcher!*

Then, as Curly quietened down, the room heard a squeaking noise as Stark swivelled on his rusty stool to face Shane. No longer wearing a jacket, his handgun was clearly visible, protruding from his waistband.

Eyeing Shane up and down, the Scotsman announced, 'He's bluffing!'

Another tense, anus puckering moment ensued as the two warriors each tried to stare the other out, neither daring to blink. Then, Shane noticed Stark's hand edging closer to his gun. So, without hesitation, he jerked his head forward in a tossing motion, releasing the grenade from its pin, which immediately caused most in the bar to cower and scream. Landing beyond the deceased's corpse, it wobbled and rolled, ending up under Stark's barstool. 'You're right!' replied Shane after spitting the pin out. And what unfolded next seemed to happen in a blur: after taking advantage of the distraction, Shane raised his arms rapidly and blasted a 9mm neatly through Stark's temple before he had even reached his weapon; then, unfortunately for Curly, as he made a sudden movement – merely to wipe away more splattered blood from himself – Shane blew a great big messy hole through his chest with the remaining slug in his shotgun. And if Red had still been standing behind him, as he had only a moment ago, he'd have copped it too! Somewhat fortunate for him, when Shane released the grenade, he fainted and fell to the floor.

Two bullets then whizzed past Shane, one after the other. Tossing the spent shotgun down, the war veteran hastily drew his attention to those on his right: Morgan was charging and screaming at him with a machete raised above his head, having relinquished his handgun to the boss; Fletcher was now desperately climbing over the top of the bar after the gun jammed on his third attempt at killing him; and the two remaining blokes at the table were now hiding under it (it turns out that they'd only come in for a quiet drink).

Without thinking twice, Shane immediately put two bullets into Morgan's Herculean chest, neutralising him in an instant, before he had a chance to bring the razor-sharp blade down upon him. However, his relief at surviving yet another close shave (pun intended) was only short-lived. As he watched his giant-size adversary crash to the floor, Fletcher suddenly came into view, standing behind the bar with a don't-fuck-with-me pump-action shotgun now in his possession!

Meanwhile, the two blokes under the table thought it would be a good idea to make a run for it while everyone else was distracted with killing each other. But as Shane dived out of Fletcher's line of fire, the two hapless, frightened men got caught in his barrage of bullets as they attempted to flee. There was blood everywhere and, needless to say, the pair died of their terrible wounds almost instantly.

Coming to that very moment and seeing the two men being blown apart, Red promptly fainted again.

Rolling onto his back, Shane fired a few rapid shots back at Fletcher, hitting his left shoulder and shattering the large mirror behind him. *'Argh!'* he yelled in pain as the bullet tore through his flesh and large shards of glass pierced through the back of his shirt. Spotting Shane, he aimed his shotgun at him and pulled the trigger. But to Fletcher's dismay, he was out of ammo! Screaming, 'FUCK!' Fletcher dropped the weapon on the bar surface with a loud clunk, then he dropped to the floor before any more of Shane's bullets found their target. Scrambling on his hands and knees, he frantically searched among the broken glass for the handgun he'd left by his feet only moments ago. Then, he noticed Atkey, crawling speedily away with it farther along the bar. 'Oi! Come back with that, you thieving little *fucker!*' he barked at once, amid the sound of gunfire, but the scrawny little barmen ignored him and continued to exit the bar.

Sitting with his back against the refrigerator, injured and exhausted, Fletcher was about to surrender when he suddenly realised there were two lots of gunfire. '... *Red!*' he spontaneously and somewhat buoyantly mouthed before yelling excitedly, 'KILL HIM, RED!'

'DON'T CHA WORRY, BOSS! I'VE GOT 'IM PINNED DOWN!' came Red's immediate reply as he fired his old, reconditioned pistol from behind an upturned round table.

Between the gunshots, sirens blared out along the top road as emergency services raced towards the blazing new development site.

Striding through the café with the pistol held firmly at his side, Will Atkey yelled, 'MELISSA!' He entered the kitchen, but he couldn't find her there either. Then he heard noises from within the storeroom. Rushing towards it, and putting an ear against the door, among the squelching and slapping sounds, he immediately recognised his wife's voice: 'Fuck me harder!' she moaned in ecstasy.

Without hesitation, Atkey sharply turned the door

handle and shoved it wide open. And there she was, knickers down, being fucked from behind by the chef. Her poor devoted husband long suspected the pair were at it, but he didn't want to believe it.

With his enormous cock rammed right up her tiny white arse, Mr Weir looked at Atkey with sweat pouring off his face and could only muster up one word: 'Shit!' Atkey's wife uttered something similar.

Atkey felt numb. 'How could you?!' he said with a strange calm, raising the handgun. It looked massive in his small, trembling hand. He pointed it at her head and then her lover's as if he couldn't decide who to kill first.

'Don't shoot!' he heard her beg.

He pulled the trigger, blowing half of Weir's head right off and spraying the small confines of the room with blood and brain tissue. The gun worked that time! Melisa screamed as she watched it slowly drip down the wall in front of her, trapped in position as she lay over the bags of spuds; then screamed even louder at the morbid realisation that the half-headless corpse was still inside her, not to mention the fear that she would be next.

Closing his glazed eyes, he aimed the gun in her direction and fired several shots. The first bullet hit her in the thigh. She screamed in pain. The second one missed. And, opening one eye, this time, he aimed at her head, killing her instantly! Then, without delay, lest he change his mind, he shoved the barrel in his mouth and blew his brains out.

Shane heard the gunshots but was too preoccupied to give them much thought because he was still in a fierce gunfight of his own.

Quickly taking cover behind an upturned table on the other side of the room from Red, Shane quickly reloaded another magazine and then continued firing. But, with so many obstacles in the way, it was nigh on impossible to get a clear shot. So, he decided to use a tactic to draw his enemy out into the open. Waiting for the next bullet to pierce the table, Shane feigned a painful death cry – which, if his head had been a few more inches to the left, would've been for real – then refrained from shooting.

Red fired one more shot. Then, after a tense moment, he yelled excitedly, 'BOSS! I THINK I GOT 'IM!'

Red's boss didn't respond.

Pointing his gun continually at Shane's position, Red dared to step around the bullet-ridden table he'd used as cover and move tentatively towards his unresponsive foe. '... Boss! Did you hear me?' he asked nervously as he stepped over dead bodies and shoved damaged chairs aside. Still, there was silence. 'BOSS! Are you all right?!' Red turned his head toward the bar as he said it. Big mistake! Peering through one of the large bullet holes Red had made, the experienced fighter immediately seized his opportunity and, springing to action, rose above the table's edge and fired a bullet straight through Red's head. His lifeless body crumpled to the floor and fell among the entanglement of corpses.

An eerie silence prevailed.

Eager to finish what he started, Shane moved swiftly towards the bar to eliminate Fletcher. But when he boldly leant over it, poised ready to shoot, he was surprised to see that he wasn't there! Immediately cocking one leg onto the bar, he slid his weary body over to the other side and, moving stealthily, followed the trail of speckled blood. 'He can't have got far!' he told himself.

Once out of the bar, the blood trail led him as far as the brightly lit kitchen, where he soon discovered the three dead staff members, explaining the other gunshots he had heard. But, strangely, no sign of a gun, nor of Fletcher!

Then, Shane noticed the emergency exit at the far end was ajar. So, with no time to ponder, he headed straight for it. Barging the door wide open, he rushed out into the darkness and the relentless rain in search of the fugitive.

The rear security light had long ceased to work, which didn't help. However, once his eyes had adjusted, beyond the small car park, he saw Fletcher's silhouette reaching almost the top of a large sand dune. He was panting heavily and clutching his injured and bloodied shoulder with the bartender's bunched-up apron.

'FLETCHER!' Shane yelled as he sprinted after him across the virtually empty car park.

A shot rang out from Fletcher's gun, missing Shane and smashing the rear window of one of the few parked cars (not that anyone inside Grafton's would be driving it any longer). Reaching the far end of the car park, the hero fired back, peppering the sand around his target until one bullet hit his right thigh. Fletcher screamed in agony, immediately dropping his weapon, before tumbling back down to the bottom of the steep slope. And there, Shane was waiting for him, constantly pointing his Glock 17 at the lowlife's head. His snarl revealed his contempt for the developer. He placed his boot firmly on the injured man's leg wound, pinning him down. Fletcher screamed in pain again. 'Damn you!' he groaned as the rain ran off of them. 'Why?! Why do you care?!'

''cos, somebody has to care and stand up for the underdog – the little guy!'

'You fuckin' cu—' began Fletcher before Shane released the rest of his magazine into him, killing him on the spot.

Putting his gun away, Shane made haste around the side of the building to rejoin his horse. 'There, there, girl. I told you everything would be all right!' he said as he unleashed Besty. Placing his boot in the stirrup, Shane slowly mounted her, his body aching from head to toe, but thankful he'd survived the gunfight unscathed, and the nightmare was now over.

Pulling the reins gently to the right, he steered her towards the road. One last glance towards the Traveller community revealed the new development was still fiercely alight, illuminating the night sky. He would miss the Starretts and the rest of the friends he'd made that summer. But it was time to head in the opposite direction. Time to leave. Then, he felt a sharp pain in his left thigh! Then another on his left side! The nightmare was not yet over! Stabbing him with long kitchen knives and screaming incessant abuse were the ugly sisters. 'You caused our boyfriend to leave us, you fuckin' bastard!' said the frenzied pair in unison, filled with hatred and rage. He felt the coldness of the blades upon each strike but was helpless against the sudden attack. 'You could've had me!' he then heard one of them garble, horrified at the thought.

In the commotion, Betsy became spooked and rose high on her hind legs, knocking one of the attackers to the ground with great force. Her head smashed against a large rock with a sickening sound. And judging by her stillness, the contorted position of her head, and her tongue hanging out, there was no doubt in Shane's mind that she had broken her neck and was dead. The other one screamed again and went to stab him a second time. Suddenly, there was a loud bang, and her head left her shoulders.

At first, Shane couldn't believe his eyes: stepping out of the shadows, dressed in his little cowboy outfit, was Bob Starrett, holding a pistol in front of him. 'Bob!' Shane called out in shocked surprise from his lofty height atop the horse. Then, a larger figure appeared from behind the boy, brandishing a smoking hunting rifle. It was the frail old ex-serviceman he'd seen in the café.

'Thank you,' said Shane once he'd calmed the horse down, relieved it wasn't Bob who'd fired the shots.

'Go!' advised the old man. 'Before the cops get here!'

Shane removed the sheriff's badge from his rain-soaked jacket and, leaning towards the boy, said slightly breathlessly, 'Here lad – you'd better have this. You're the sheriff in town now!'

Shane then heard Marian's voice calling her son's name farther up the road. 'Go to your mum, Bobby-boy,' he said caringly. 'She'll be worried about you!'

Both veterans then saluted one another and, gently tapping his heels against the horse, the hero of this story trotted away.

'Shane, you're going the wrong way!' Bob suddenly called out, finding his voice.

'Go to your mum!' he repeated in pain as he picked up the pace to a gallop.

'BUT SHANE! YOU'RE HURT!' the concerned boy yelled as he ran along the road after him. 'COME BACK, SHANE! SHANE COME BACK ...!' The boy stopped. 'ALRIGHT – PISS OFF THEN!'

THE END

ACKNOWLEDGEMENTS

A big thank you to the artist, Jason M, for so splendidly turning my idea for the book cover's design into a reality!

www.ingramcontent.com/pod-product-compliance
Lightning Source LLC
LaVergne TN
LVHW050957080826
845145LV00009B/2331

* 9 7 8 1 7 3 9 2 3 5 5 8 1 *